Praise for the Ava Logan Mystery Series

"Well-drawn characters, a dash of romance, and enough logically constructed red herrings to keep the reader guessing right up to the end distinguish this tightly woven tale."

– *Publishers Weekly*

"The first in Willis' planned series mixes murder and romance with enough suspects to keep you guessing."

– *Kirkus Reviews*

"As a reader who loves intricate mysteries that are filled to the brim with investigations, I'm grateful there will be more to come."

– *Suspense Magazine*

"A well-wrought tale of the secrets concealed beneath the surface of small-town Appalachia...Willis is a seasoned professional who gives us just enough red herrings to keep us guessing to the end."

— Margaret Maron,
New York Times Bestselling Author of *Long Upon the Land*

"A page-turning balance of small-town life and an unsolvable mystery with characters we wish we knew for real. *Tell Me No Lies* is a mystery that will not disappoint."

– C. Hope Clark,
Author of *Echoes of Edisto*

"Willis brings to life not only the beauty of the Appalachia, but also the crippling poverty that can and does cause people to resort to terrible things."

– *For the Love of Books*

"Lynn Chandler Willis writes with a voice as big as the Appalachians. *Tell Me No Lies* is a compelling mystery and a spot-on depiction of newspapering in a small town. I'm already looking forward to more from Ava Logan."

– Brad Parks,
Shamus, Nero, and Lefty Award-Winning Author of *Say Nothing*

"A pulse-pounding treat with a coiling plot. This one provides intelligent and intriguing thrills about love, loyalty, and courage. Way ahead of the pack."

– Steve Berry,
New York Times #1 and International Bestselling Author

"*Tell Me No Secrets* has it all—strong, unforgettable characters, a beautiful setting, dark secrets, and a haunting story that rises like a deadly storm out of the turbulent borderland between love and faith, the modern world, and traditional Appalachian culture."

— Roger Johns,
Award-Winning Author of the Wallace Hartman Mysteries

"Willis weaves a gripping and lush tale of big city crime colliding with backwoods folklore where the secrets are as dark and mysterious as the Appalachian Mountains. Ava Logan is the kind of sympathetic but strong heroine who juggles a demanding job with the struggles of family life...someone we can all relate to and cheer for. I was drawn in from the very first page, desperately wanted to find out what happened, but hated to see it come to an end."

— Annette Dashofy,
USA Today Bestselling Author of the Zoe Chambers Mystery Series

TELL ME NO SECRETS

The Ava Logan Mystery Series by Lynn Chandler Willis

TELL ME NO LIES (#1)
TELL ME NO SECRETS (#2)
TELL ME YOU LOVE ME (#3)

TELL ME NO SECRETS

AN AVA LOGAN MYSTERY

LYNN CHANDLER WILLIS

HENERY PRESS

Copyright

TELL ME NO SECRETS
An Ava Logan Mystery
Part of the Henery Press Mystery Collection

First Edition | June 2019

Henery Press, LLC
www.henerypress.com

Trade Paperback ISBN-13: 978-1-63511-519-2
Digital epub ISBN-13: 978-1-63511-520-8
Kindle ISBN-13: 978-1-63511-521-5
Hardcover ISBN-13: 978-1-63511-522-2

Printed in the United States of America

For my granddaughter, Paisley.
I love you more.

ACKNOWLEDGMENTS

My unyielding gratitude goes to Karen Fritz, Micki Bare, and Julie Bates for helping me craft this idea into an actual story. Thank you for the brainstorming sessions and the multiple cups of coffee. Thank you, Cindy Cipriano Bullard, for keeping me on track and pushing me forward. Thank you to Agnes Alexander (Lynette Hall Hampton) for being my mentor, teacher, and friend. A huge thank you to my sister, Rae Chandler, for the road trips we called research and for being okay with turning down all those little mountain roads.

And to the people of Appalachia, thank you for your openness and warm welcome. I hope I did good in this portrayal.

CHAPTER 1

People don't just disappear. Unless they do.

To begin with, Scott Curry's no-show for work Thursday more than worried me. In the three years he'd been delivering the *Jackson Creek Chronicle*, he'd never skipped work. But when he didn't show or call this past delivery day, his absence at first created more of an inconvenience than concern. As publisher of the town's only newspaper, I had no choice but deliver the papers myself.

That was three days ago. The mild concern had grown into serious worry. No calls, no emails, no texts combined with a gnawing feeling *something's wrong.* Jackson County Sheriff Grayson Ridge chewed on the end of a shank of grass plucked from the river bank, slowly twirling the other end between his thumb and index finger while I expressed my concern. He ditched the grass then tucked a wayward strand of auburn hair behind my ear. His way of showing me he was at least listening.

His other arm rested at my waist, his fingers laced through the belt loops of my capris. We sat with my son Cole and my two-year-old adopted daughter Ivy on a blanket spread over a patch of grass about thirty feet from the river's edge, watching a baptism. My twelve-year-old daughter, Emma, along with other believers were making their faith public today. I, myself, was a more private believer.

I pushed the thoughts of bad things and Scott Curry out of my head and tried to escape into the jovial mood, into the beauty of the surrounding mountains, but came up short. Although a pleasant seventy-eight degrees, seeing the line of believers standing in that cold river made me shiver. I studied the scene a moment, wondering where they found the courage to do it. To allow the chilled water to swirl around them. To profess their faith.

Waist-deep in the muddy water of Jackson Creek, Reverend Doretha Andrews lifted her arms toward the heavens shouting praise in a language I didn't understand. Latin? Or maybe Hebrew. From a cloudless, Carolina blue sky, the sun illuminated her face, tears glistening against her ebony skin. Tears of joy? Had to be. She loved saving souls and the fact one of those souls belonged to my daughter–an added bonus.

The water ebbed and flowed around the reverend, lifting her baptismal robe. The purple garment swirled with the current, splaying on the surface, Doretha anchoring it in place.

She'd been my anchor the better part of twenty-seven years. When I was eight, my mother blasted my father to hell with a shotgun and became a resident at the North Carolina Women's Prison in Raleigh so Doretha took me in to the All Faith Missionary foster home. A big bosomed lady with swinging braids, Doretha preached the gospel with a soft voice and gentle manner...except when it came to baptizing new believers. She then became so engulfed with the spirit you'd fully expect Jesus Christ himself to open the heavens, swoop down to the river and hug her.

Now, with the church's band and choir making a joyful noise on the bank of Jackson Creek, Emma waited to be dipped along with six others. Each of those waiting in line swayed hypnotically to the thumping of the bongo as the water swirled around them. Any other day, my own shoulders would have moved involuntarily to the rhythm of the fiddle, the twang of the banjo. But not today. Not when my instincts whispered something was wrong. It wasn't like Scott to miss work.

"He has a sister in Ohio," I said in a hushed tone. "Maybe we can check with her."

Grayson glanced in my direction, the exact destination of his line of sight skewed by his Oakleys. "I've got a call in to his parents. Hopefully we'll hear something tomorrow."

Cole huffed, the universal sign of teenage boredom. "Mom, I told you—school's been out three weeks. He's at the beach partying."

Maybe he was right. Being the middle of May, the grade schools still had a few weeks left, but Brighton College had closed its doors for the summer. Although late spring in the North Carolina high country competed in beauty with the autumn, college kids found more joy in hot sand, waves and endless beer on the other side of the state than in the flowering rhododendron and mountain laurel of home. Aside from being a college kid, Scott was also an avid hiker and backpacker. Even if he didn't go to the beach, he could be on a trail somewhere, off the grid for a few days. But surely he would have carried his cell. If he was somewhere he couldn't get a signal out, he'd have let someone know where he would be, what trail he was hiking. That was rule one of the outdoors.

With Emma still in line, I looked away from the baptism, glancing around the hollow. Clusters of wildflowers surrounded our spot at the river, giving the gentle slope a splash of color and sweet aroma. Though the water from the creek emanated a musty smell, it was home. It was roots and family.

About forty of us—Doretha's past and present foster kids—gathered every year in late spring at this same spot for a reunion and baptism service. Those with partners or spouses or kids brought them along to share in the occasion, strengthening the ties that made us family.

Those waiting in line to be baptized, like Emma, pulled at their robes, clutching them at their sides to keep the material from floating to the top of the water. Some of the children giggled as they let their frocks rise only to tug them back down to their sides.

My red-headed Emma fidgeted with her gown as well. She was a good kid, more mature than her twelve years. She'd taken on the role of big sister naturally last fall when I'd adopted Ivy after her own mother died.

From the distance, I saw Emma studying the brownish-orange mud line marring her white robe. I wanted to tell her it would be alright. Like the supposed sin she felt she'd accumulated in her twelve short years, the stain would wash away.

She'd convinced me to let her be baptized. Not that I opposed it; I just wasn't convinced a pre-teen could comprehend the true meaning. I wasn't even sure I understood it. Perhaps Emma had fallen more under Doretha's preaching than I had.

As I watched the water flow downstream, my thoughts flowed back to Scott. If he had a reason to want to disappear, I didn't know it. I saw him every Thursday at the office when we transferred the bundles of papers from the printer's van to his beat-up SUV. We chatted about the weather and about school. A junior at Brighton, the next step was Wake Forest law school. He had plans.

Cole sighed again then tickled Ivy, pinching at her chubby thighs. "How long do we have to stay? I'm supposed to meet Paisley later."

Apparently Scott wasn't the only one who had alternative plans. "We're staying until it's over."

Ivy's giggle turned into an unfiltered laugh, drawing attention to our spot. Even Doretha looked at us from her location in the river. She smiled and lifted her arms in praise, for the children, the laughter, or the spirit moving her. Who knew? It was just a part of who she was.

Cole ducked the attention and lay back on the blanket. He shielded his eyes from the blaring sun with his forearm. "Why doesn't Doretha baptize people in one of those little pool things like other churches?"

I dug a bag of fruit snacks from Ivy's diaper bag, handing them to her in hopes she'd settle back down. "They're called baptismal pools, and All Faith Missionary Church doesn't have one. Besides, there's something very symbolic about being baptized in a river."

"Were you baptized in a river?"

"No," I said, probably too quickly. As the water pushed over an outcrop of tree roots. Pudge Collins' beagles howled up the river a way, the mournful cry echoing off the rocks.

Cole watched me, waiting for me to elaborate. When I didn't, his interest returned to his teenage hormones. "So what am I supposed to tell Paisley?"

"You can tell her you'll see her at school tomorrow."

I swear he growled then turned to Grayson, his male ally. "Help me out here."

Grayson snickered, his fingers pulling tighter around my waist. "You're on your own with this one. You know how she is."

Square-jawed, with rich chocolate-colored hair, broad shoulders on a solid frame, Cole resembled his late father more every day. But I wouldn't hold that against him. While my dead husband had pretended to protect and serve, behind closed doors he beat me black and blue to match his uniform. When a bullet shredded his aorta ten years ago during a routine call, I mourned for my two small children and I mourned for the happily-ever-after life I'd always wanted. But I didn't mourn for Tommy.

A roar of laughter erupted from the river, spreading up to the crowd on the bank. The sound jerked my focus back to the baptism where I'd already missed the joke.

"Earth to Ava Logan," Grayson said, his voice low, his gaze penetrating even through his sunglasses. "You okay?"

I answered with the truth. "No. I'm really worried about Scott. It's so out of character."

He playfully nudged my shoulder. "You're just mad because you had to deliver the papers."

There might have been a smidgen of truth in that statement. As the founder of the *Jackson Creek Chronicle*, I'd spent my time delivering. I climbed in and out of a vehicle more on delivery day than I did an entire year. Once the paper could afford a small staff, I hired a delivery driver first. Scott Curry wasn't my original driver, but he was the best.

Cole pointed at Doretha and the baptism party. "Looks like Emma's after the next girl. Can we leave after that?"

Grayson turned away to hide his grin while I shot my son a momma look. "We're not leaving, Cole."

I forced Scott from my mind, giving my full attention to the service. Doretha placed one hand behind the head of a young man, the other hand on his chest. "Jesus answered, truly, truly, I say to you, except a man be born of water and of the spirit, he cannot enter into the kingdom of God."

With help from Elder Jeremiah Carson, she lowered the boy into the muddy water, framing his upper body with her arms.

He came up sputtering a little, a broad smile spreading across his face. "Praise God!" he shouted, giving a fist pump high in the air.

Doretha laughed from her belly, a comforting sound, that always made me smile no matter the situation.

"Bet that water's cold." Cole dug at the soft earth with a stick.

Even in mid-summer when the air temperature reached nineties, the river water in the North Carolina mountains usually missed the memo. "I imagine it's very cold," I said.

"Frigid is more like it," Grayson added.

The next girl stepped up to Doretha. She folded her arms across her chest, visibly shaking. Probably more from the cool water than nerves. Emma moved up in line. In my lap, Ivy pointed a chubby finger toward Emma, calling her "Emem."

Emma wiggled her fingers in a tiny wave at us. But when she turned back toward Doretha, her gaze stopped up river, brows knitted. A frown pulled at her lips. I followed her gaze, focusing on something floating downstream to where they stood. Emma turned back to us, lifting her shoulders in a shrug. Whatever floated in the water had lost its appeal to my daughter. But not to me. Too wide to be a snake. An injured beaver or otter? A turtle maybe? Whatever it was, it was headed straight for my daughter.

With growing concern, I handed Ivy off to Grayson and slowly stood to get a better look.

Emma shook her head in my direction, a silent plea to not embarrass her. My heart rate increased the closer I stepped toward the water. A green and black backpack rose and fell like a fishing bobber on the move. A backpack just like Scott's.

I skittered down the riverbank, a clumsy splash screaming my plunge into the river. My breath hitched as ice cold water pierced my capris, stabbing my legs like needles as I struggled against the current. The bongo player stopped tapping out a beat. The fiddle player brought his bow to a screeching halt.

"Mom, what are you doing?" Emma yelled.

I lunged for the backpack before it drifted farther downstream, covered to my waist in the freezing water.

"Ava!" Doretha shouted.

Adrenaline rushed through my blood like the river rushing over the rocks. My heart raced with fear of what I'd found. I couldn't stop my body from shaking as I towed the bag toward the shore.

Struggling to find my footing on the slippery bank, anxious to get out of the freezing water, I shoved my free hand at Grayson, allowing him to yank me from the river's clutches.

I tossed the water-logged backpack to the ground. Breathless, I managed, "It's Scott's."

CHAPTER 2

From a few yards away, a crowd watched Grayson poke around the backpack. They stood at a distance as if scared something would jump out. I forced my focus on the bag to keep from shivering from the chill. The water temperature of the river had yet to catch up with the warmth of the late spring air and my wet clothes weren't helping.

Grayson removed the bladder pack then a compass, a trail map safely tucked into a waterproof case, a pair of wool socks still dry in a plastic baggie, a protein snack, and a first aid kit. Everything an experienced hiker like Scott would carry. Grayson opened a smaller compartment then removed an I.D. case. He glanced up at me before opening it.

I wrapped my arms around myself, hoping to quieten the shivers, and stared at the river. I didn't need to see the I.D. to know it was Scott's.

Grayson blew a heavy sigh as he stood, wiping his wet hands on his jeans. He pushed a clump of coal-black hair from his eyes with his forearm then called for Doretha.

With the hem of her sopping wet robe clutched in her hands, she joined us near the edge of the water.

"We've got a situation. I hate it but we're going to have to stop the service," Grayson said.

When confusion narrowed her eyes, I offered, "My delivery guy didn't show Thursday. That's his day pack."

She jerked her head around to stare at me, shielding her eyes from the sun with her water-wrinkled hand. "Oh Lord. You thinking something happened to him?"

I nodded. "We don't know what exactly, but I don't have a good feeling."

Grayson looked around at the crowd. "I'm going to call for a K9 unit. Doretha, would you mind taking the kids with you?"

Doretha shook her head, her braids clicking against one another. "Of course not. But is there anything we can do here to help?

I looked up the bank at Emma standing at our blanket with Cole and Ivy. The dripping robe hung on her shoulders, her excitement drained. My heart ached, knowing the disappointment she felt. For weeks, this baptism dominated her life and to have it so dramatically interrupted by her own mother had to sting.

I'd make it up to her somehow. But right now, a missing twenty-one-year-old delivery boy needed my full attention.

Elder Jeremiah Carson emerged from the crowd and came over to us. It didn't take an investigative reporter to know his role in the church was more than just an elder. And I think he resented me for knowing. "Doretha, the people want to know what we're gonna do. Are we gonna finish the service?"

Doretha wrapped her arm around my shoulder, giving me a gentle squeeze. "Not today, Jeremiah. We'll reschedule. Will you gather everyone for a word of prayer, please?"

Jeremiah glanced at the backpack then at me with a

stinging glare. The feeling was mutual but petty jealousies weren't my biggest concern at the moment. "Of course."

After he returned to the worshipers, Doretha turned to Grayson. "Maybe, rather than have everyone leave, we could help search. We can walk the river bank in pairs."

Grayson thought about it while studying the river. "I appreciate it, but too many people can throw the K9 off scent. If you want to wait until he's through, I'll have a deputy help organize a search party."

Despite the foreboding nature of the moment, my hope raised. At least now Scott would have people looking for him. Wherever he was, or whatever happened, at least there were people who cared.

Now with a mission, Doretha hurried up the hill to gather her troops. With her staying, that meant my kids were staying, too. "I should help Emma get into some dry clothes."

Grayson reached for my hand as I turned to leave. "You need some dry clothes, too. Why don't you—"

"I'm not going home. I'm good." I added a smile to convince him. "Promise."

I trekked up the hill to the kids where Cole met me with impatience. "Can we leave now?"

"We're not going anywhere for a while. And Doretha's going to be keeping an eye on y'all while we're here." Ivy tugged on my wet pants, wanting me to pick her up. I didn't need her wet, too, so did my best to put her off.

Cole exhaled strong enough to flutter the leaves. "Mom. Seriously?"

"Yes. Seriously. Play with Ivy while I help Emma change."

Emma, still stunned, made no effort to move. "What do you think happened to Scott?"

I didn't want to lie to her, but I didn't want to cause more worry either. "Not sure. Hopefully we'll have some answers soon. Let's get you into some dry clothes."

She didn't argue, just turned and headed to the back of the Tahoe. Shoulders slumped. Empty.

I dug a set of dry clothes from the bag she'd packed for after what was supposed to be her baptism. While I held an old quilt up to block unwanted eyes, she changed into a pair of shorts and a t-shirt. If I'd known I'd have been wading chest deep in the river, I wouldn't have worn a white t-shirt.

"Do you think something bad happened to Scott?" She asked, her voice small.

I wanted to wrap her in the quilt to shield her from the world and all its uncertainties. Although I loved her sensitivity, her vulnerability worried me. But I didn't lie to her. "Let's hope for the best."

She slowly nodded like it required effort.

Cole whined from around the front of the truck. "Mom, how much longer do I have to hold Ivy? She's getting heavy."

Now dressed, Emma rolled her eyes. "I'll get her," she whispered. And just like that, my daughter was back with a purpose.

I wrapped her in a tight hug, kissing the top of her gorgeous red hair. "Thank you. Y'all go on over to the church van and hang out with Doretha."

Cole gladly handed Ivy to his sister then huffed about every teenage crisis to plague his life as he stomped over to the church van.

I searched the Tahoe for an old shirt. Dirt-smeared or oil-stained had to be better than wet and white. Two diapers, a dozen petrified French fries, and a Disney movie DVD. Any other time, there'd be an extra jacket or two. Going home to grab dry clothes wasn't an option; I'd just have to deal with it.

When I got back over to Grayson, the K9 unit was en route. Grayson had removed the trail map from the protective case, spreading it on the ground.

"That's Spearhead Mountain," I said. The kids and I had hiked it a few times. Not enough to know it in detail. Known for an abundance of arrowheads, the trail was rated easy to moderate. A four-mile loop. Well below Scott's level. He could have hiked it easily, but the proximity didn't make sense. "That trail isn't anywhere near the river."

Crouching, Grayson pointed to a spot on the map. "But look. The southeast portion of the loop comes within a mile of the water."

He stood and studied the terrain, getting his bearings. We shared many things, but the love of hiking wasn't one of them. His idea of sport involved bases, a bat and glove.

He pointed upstream. "The trail head would be...Northwest? That'd be the most logical place to start."

While Grayson made another call, a flock of birds flapped in the trees then scattered, their feathers ruffled as much as the pine branches they flew from. The suddenness of their flight jerked my attention away from the moment. Startled, my heart grabbed in my chest. "Jiminy," I mumbled, having taken up identifying a cricket rather than talking like a sailor.

Grayson turned his eyes to me as he slipped his phone in his pocket. "You okay?"

I didn't know how to answer. I was cold, tired, and worried. "I'll be a lot better when we find him."

"Maness is going to meet us at the trail head with Ruger. I'll have Sullivan stay here to help organize a search on this side."

I followed him up the hill where he went straight to Doretha. Like Emma, she had changed into dry clothes, too. I wondered if Elder Jeremiah Carson held a blanket up for her. "Steve Sullivan will be here shortly. He'll help you organize a search. Until he gets here, I'm asking everyone to stay right here. We're meeting the K9 unit across the river."

"Can I go with y'all?" Cole asked, his sudden concern a rue. I knew my son too well. He was probably hoping we could drop him off at home on our way.

"No," Grayson and I said in unison. A united front.

"I need you to stay here and help with Ivy," I added.

Ivy wiggled against Emma, reaching for me, her chubby fingers squeezing air. Doretha took the toddler, bouncing her in her arms. "Ya'll go. We got this side of the river covered."

I gave Ivy a quick kiss and hugged Emma extra-long, still feeling a twinge of guilt over her ruined baptism. I'd make it up to her. Somehow.

I turned off Crest View Road, easing the Tahoe into the gravel parking lot marking the entrance to Spearhead mountain. An older model Jeep with the top off, a spit-shined Ford pickup, and a family sedan parked far enough apart to not invade the other's space. An old-style bicycle leaned against the split-rail fence separating the parking lot and the trail head. The bike belonged to Keeper McCarter, a local everyone knew. Most protected him. Others avoided him.

A man and woman with two kids enjoyed a picnic at one of the wooden tables near the tree line. The kids looked around six and seven, the age where they still thought mom and dad knew everything.

Grayson's baritone voice jerked me out of my imagination. "Would Scott have parked in the parking lot?"

Scott drove a well-traveled S.U.V. and it wasn't here. "He would have to. Unless he came with someone else." The trail lay miles from Scott's off-campus apartment, too far for a casual stroll. But not too far to need a daypack.

Deputy Jeff Maness pulled into the parking lot behind us in a black SUV marked in white with *Jackson County Sheriff Department K9 Unit—Stay Back*. The mom and dad at the picnic table shared a worried look.

A spark of adrenaline reignited my energy. I hopped out of the Tahoe, rearranging my damp clothes. Maness was out of his vehicle leashing Ruger, a Belgian Malinois. While Grayson filled him in, I watched the mother and father scurrying their children into their car. Dad hurried to clean up the picnic supplies while mom moved the frightened kids toward the sedan. I wanted to apologize for interrupting their picnic, their family time. My own daughter's baptism, an innocent family's picnic...what else could I interrupt today?

Grayson handed Maness the bagged socks from the backpack. The dog popped with excitement, the desire to lunge as clear as the concern on the picnicking mother's face. Maness held the socks down in front of Ruger then released the tension on the leash.

The shepherd headed straight for the trail with Maness in tow. Grayson and I hurried to catch up. Two years shy of forty, Grayson Ridge was in his second term as sheriff of Jackson County, and as popular as a high school quarterback. He'd been my dead husband's patrol partner when Tommy was killed in the line of duty. He'd shouldered as much guilt as I had at Tommy's death. We had history.

In sneakers, wet sneakers at that, rather than my hiking boots, my heels rubbed against the canvas. A blister'd be forming soon. I pushed through a low hanging pine branch, inhaling the sweet scent of the sticky sap.

About a mile in, Ruger alerted, leading off the trail. Briers snagged at my legs, scratching and tearing flesh as we followed. Grayson pushed ahead of me, trying to fend off the painful vines.

I usually found solace in the forest, but not today. An unease amplified each sound, giving the woods a sinister feel. Every creak of a twig snapping caught my attention. Every flash of sunlight filtering through trees reminded me of a spotlight, with that moment of temporary blindness and a second's worth of panic at fearing what was beyond the brilliance.

With Maness and Ruger several yards ahead of us, my heart raced at the sound of a scream followed by Ruger's frenzied bark. Grayson jerked the Glock from the waistband of his jeans with one hand, and with the other jerked me behind him.

Within seconds, we caught up to Maness and Ruger, and Keeper McCarter.

Keeper, a look of sheer panic splashed across his face, stood with his arms reaching high in the air, a metal rod in each hand.

"Ain't doing nuthin', Sheriff Ridge. I promise," he stuttered. He quickly shook his head to emphasis his point. His fifty-year-old face filling with the shame and fear of a seven-year-old. Keeper McCarter was known throughout the hills and hollers surrounding Jackson Creek as being simple-minded. He lived with his mother Mary and swept floors at the fire station for money to buy the occasional orange soda.

Grayson, gun still in hand, stepped in front of Maness. "What are you doing out here, Keeper? Why are you this far off the trail?"

Keeper lowered his arms and stared at the metal rods in his hands like he just remembered they were there. "I was playing around with these. I fount 'em in the old barn out back. They was my pawpaw's."

The thin rods, rusted where white enamel paint had chipped off, looked like an old wire coat hanger straightened then snipped in two.

I stepped forward, hoping my presence was less intimidating. Poor guy, with his child-like mind, had to be terrified. "What are those, Keeper?"

He looked them over again then squared his shoulders, more sure of himself. "Dowsing rods."

"You dowsing for water?" Grayson asked.

"Oh no sir. These ain't water dowsing rods. These are grave dowsing rods."

CHAPTER 3

I couldn't take my eyes off the two rods in Keeper's hands. I'd heard whispers of grave dowsing but hadn't witnessed it. Spoken of in hushed conversations like sharing secrets, folklore lived and breathed in these hills as an entity all its own.

A chill still skirted up my back. "What makes you think there's a grave around here, Keeper?"

His eyes searched the ground between us, an unease growing. Ruger kept barking, aggressive and threatening. "I gotta git home. Momma'll be looking for me."

Grayson's breath was warm against my neck as he spoke, his tone softer than before. "Keeper, whose grave are you looking for?"

Keeper's focus darted around the woods, avoiding direct eye contact with either of us. Although the six-foot, muscular frame of a grown man stood a few feet from me, the mind of child struggled for words. "Charly's. They said they buried him out here."

"Who said they buried him out here?" Grayson asked.

Maness finally got Ruger to quieten, though the dog continued to whine with impatience.

"I gotta go," Keeper said, eyes scanning his surroundings.

Grayson spoke in a voice as soft as butter. "Keeper—who buried Charly out here in the woods?"

Keeper nudged at the ground with the toe of his well-worn boot. "They told me not to tell. It's a secret."

I met Grayson's eyes, unsure of where to go next with the questions. Keeper McCarter was as harmless as a June bug but he knew something that scared him.

"Keeper, who is Charly?" Grayson asked, his voice steady. "Was he a friend of yours?"

Keeper hesitated then shook his head quickly, his wavy brown hair brushing side-to-side. "He was my momma's cat. He was black, and real shiny. They kilt him 'cause they said my momma's a witch."

My chest tightened, squeezing the air out of my lungs. Mary McCarter had been the subject of overzealous imaginations since she first used her gift. Killing her cat because of the gift was repulsive. I reached out for Keeper but dropped my hand when he took a step backward. "Oh, Keeper. I'm so sorry they hurt Charly. Tell us who they are so Sheriff Ridge can make sure they don't hurt anyone else's cat."

His agitation rose. "I gotta get. Momma'll be looking for me." He rushed past us disappearing into the forest, the signature blue flannel shirt fading into the landscape.

"Keeper—" I started after him, but Grayson grabbed my arm.

"Let him go. We'll talk to him later."

Ruger reminded us of his mission with an ear-splitting bark. Maness gave the dog a refresher with the wool socks then released tension on the leash. Ruger stayed off trail, leading us deeper into the woods.

Tiny fingers of the underbrush scratched my bare ankles, but I shoved forward, moving toward the river. Ribbons of sunlight flickered through the pines as if someone kept flipping the light on and off. The air turned dank, a musty smell rising from the ground. The river couldn't be far away.

Ruger lunged, pulling Maness with him down a slope. Grayson and I followed, dodging trees and underbrush while skirting down the hill to the water. Unlike where we held the baptism, woods shrouded the riverbank.

My pulse soared with apprehension, worrying what we'd find, and what we wouldn't. The rushing water roared over slick boulders and fallen trees, echoing through the holler. I navigated over roots and rocks, brushing low hanging branches out of the way.

Facing the water, Ruger pawed at the ground and whined. High-pitched, it wasn't the normal alert. An unusual uncertainty marred the dog's announcement.

I wedged myself between Grayson and a dying oak to get a better look. "What does that mean?"

Maness pulled back on the dog's leash, tugging him away from the edge of the bank. "It means he lost the scent."

Grayson pushed his fingers through his hair, a rare look of worry creasing his forehead. "The speed that water's flowing, it's no wonder the dog lost it." He stared down river, shaking his head. "It wasn't flowing anywhere near that fast where we were. It has to be dammed up somewhere."

Without waiting, I headed down river. Rushing water butted up against the natural barrier of roots and underbrush that formed the bank. A sense of urgency drove me over, under, and through the obstacle as images of a body, hung up on fallen trees, submerged, face down flashed like a strobe light through my mind.

About twenty yards into the trek, Grayson came up behind me, without Maness or Ruger. No way the dog could navigate this terrain. No real reason, too. He'd lost the scent at the edge of the water.

A good mile from where we started along the bank, we found the dam. A cluster of fallen Eastern hemlocks stretched across a narrow spot in the river. Their branches reached for the other side but came up short. Boulders the size of a small car stockpiled on the other side of the downed trees, preventing them from floating downstream. What else lay trapped by the barricade?

I'd grown up around this river, but I only knew its depth in spots. It was safe to cross with the water level knee, maybe thigh high. Where the water pooled deep enough to actually swim. I couldn't look away from the nature-made dam and the possibilities of what, or who, might be trapped under the snare.

The roar of rushing water had settled into a low drone as it slapped against the dead hemlocks. The pecking tone of Grayson's cell phone intruded on the landscape like an unwelcome visitor.

He pecked some more then cursed. "Damnit."

Finally, I peeled my eyes away from the river, stealing a glance at his phone. No bars. At that moment, that's how I felt. Empty. And useless. "Who were you calling?" I asked, my voice as tired as I felt.

He slipped his phone back into his pocket, resignation shadowing in his eyes. "Garland Phelps."

"With the fire department?"

The resignation grew and crept into his face. "With the swift water rescue and recovery team."

I gave the river one last look before we headed back to the trail head.

Back at the parking lot, Maness had already left with Ruger, their mission complete. I had mixed emotions about calling it a success. Keeper's bicycle was also gone along with the other vehicles.

I leaned against the Tahoe and waited while Grayson tried his phone again. This time, the call went through. Hearing him say the word "missing" sent images pounding through my head. I massaged my forehead hoping to rub them away.

Grayson clicked his phone off then returned it to his jean's pocket. With no one around to criticize the sheriff's public display of affection, he pulled me to him and I let him. I sank into his comfort, hoping some of his strength would seep through my own pores.

He lightly pressed his lips to my forehead. "Why don't you take the kids and go on home? This is going to take a while."

Whether exhausted or numb, my words dribbled out like a slow drip. "Have his parents been contacted?"

"I have a deputy doing it now. Sullivan and Doretha's group have searched as far as they can across the river so I'm going to send them home, too."

It sounded so final. Like, although we didn't find him, everyone knew the answer. And the answer wasn't the one I'd hoped for.

I'd regret putting Ivy down for a late nap, but no amount of coddling could defeat her crankiness. Even Emma advocated for some downtime. With Cole sulking in his bedroom, Emma studied for a science test on her iPad at the kitchen table while I fixed grilled cheese and soup for supper. Nothing like comfort food after a day like today. Finn, our border collie, waited patiently for me to toss her a piece of cheese. At my feet, her ears perked up every time I unwrapped a slice.

Emma drummed her pencil on the table in a mindless rhythm. *Tap...tap...tap*. "Eww. That's gross," she mumbled.

"What's gross?"

After a pause, she answered in a barely-there voice. "What happens to a body in water."

I jerked around, a child I didn't know in my vision. "What are you studying?" Decomposing bodies weren't in my sixth-grade curriculum. Or any curriculum.

Her mouth puckered then twisted in exaggeration. "Um...I was just curious. You know...about Scott."

The verbalization of my own question, my own fear, slammed me in the gut, nearly stealing my breath. I marched to the table and grabbed her iPad. Images flickering in a YouTube video pushed bile into my throat. The power button couldn't remove the sight fast enough. Given what she'd already seen, I was certain the visual would revisit my daughter deep in the night in the middle of her sleep.

"You don't need to be watching this," I snapped as I handed it back to her, shut down. Back at the stove, a sandwich sizzled, nearing being burnt status. "Besides, I thought you were studying."

She stared at the black screen. "I took a break."

"Well, you don't need to be looking at stuff like that."

Emma's iPad flickered back to life. She opened the school's homework helper app, settling in for what I hoped was studying for her test.

"Do you think Scott drowned?"

Apparently, her morbid curiosity wouldn't allow her to study what she was supposed to. I set the griddle off the stove, leaned against the counter and faced her. Arms folded across my chest. "Honestly, I don't know what to think, Emma. He could just be away for spring break and forgot to tell me."

She drummed her pencil again. *Tap…tap…tap.* "Spring break was two months ago."

I slammed a sandwich on a paper plate. Stirred the soup. "Okay, you need to go tell your brother supper's almost ready."

Emma huffed in true pre-teen fashion then disappeared up the stairs. Damnit! Nerves still frazzled from the river, dealing with a twelve-year-old's sudden interest in body decomp might force an early bedtime. For everyone.

After a too quiet supper, I plunked Ivy in the bathtub, threw in some of her tub toys and collapsed on the closed toilet. Emma usually helped with bath time but tonight, I didn't ask. She still had homework and it didn't involve water-logged bodies. Her search history would reveal if I could expect nightmares to keep us both up. It'd been a trying day for all of us.

I let Ivy play a few minutes then washed her hair to remove splotches of melted cheese. She threw just shy of a hissy fit. The lavender-scented baby wash wasn't very calming.

Emma bounded into the bathroom, giggling at the dramatic interpretation of a toddler's near-death experience. "Is mom trying to kill you, Ivy?"

I wasn't going to question my daughter's now chirpy mood. "Did you finish your homework?"

"Yes, ma'am. You want me to finish with Ivy?"

"Sure. You can let her play for a few more minutes if you

want." I dried my hands on Ivy's My Little Pony towel then left the two girls alone in the bathroom.

I went back downstairs and retrieved my phone from the kitchen. Finn took every step I did, following me into the sun room. Although I adored every inch of the old farm house we called home, the sun room was my sanctuary. Tommy and I had added it on after buying the house, a wall of windows overlooking the very river where Emma was supposed to have been baptized.

The same river that had claimed Scott's backpack. And maybe even Scott.

I dropped onto the cotton-soft sofa, tucking my legs underneath me. And called Grayson. "Hey," I said when he answered, surprised he had a signal. "Anything new?"

"Not really. We're packing up for tonight. Gonna do a grid search in the morning." Even his calm manner couldn't cover the tiredness in his voice. "We made contact with his family."

My stomach jerked with the sudden realization there were now others concerned with Scott's no-show for work. His parents and sister, all now given reason to worry. As a mother, my eyes moistened with sympathy for Mrs. Curry. I'd always heard the not knowing was harder than the finality.

"Ava? You there?"

I brushed away a stray tear. "Yeah. Sorry. I was just thinking how horrible it must be to not know."

His breath was slow and steady, coming over the phone in that controlled mindset of his. "Stop thinking. Get some rest. I'll talk to you in the morning, okay?"

"You'll call if you find anything, right?" I absently tugged at a loose thread winding through the seam of my pants. Unraveled. That's how I felt.

"I'll call. Love you."

"Love you, too."

I hung up then lightly petted Finn. The dog curled into the affection, pawing my leg for more.

Then a memory slammed me so hard it jolted my hand away from Finn. Scott shared his apartment with a cat. A white and brown tom named Boone. Scott had rescued the stray from sliding traffic during a heavy snow while delivering papers for me. Cats tended to be more self-sufficient than dogs, but they still needed caring for. An extra bowl of food and water could mean Scott anticipated being gone longer than just the day. And an empty bowl would mean he didn't plan on being gone at all.

CHAPTER 4

Monday morning ushered in an anxious energy. Dread sparked nerve endings I didn't know I had. The desire for Grayson to call and say they found Scott, he was fine, hanging with college pals at the beach competed with not wanting him to call at all. I didn't want to hear what I feared he *would* find.

While Cole and Emma ate their cereal of choice, I popped a bowl of oatmeal in the microwave for Ivy. This week, she preferred oatmeal. With raisins. Next week, we'd be back to PopTarts.

When I couldn't stand it any longer, I called Grayson. "Good morning."

Chatter in the background filtered through the phone. "Morning."

The stove clock showed 6:50. "Are you already at the river?"

"Yeah. The guys are suiting up."

The microwave dinged, much to Ivy's delight. She clapped then hurriedly climbed into her booster seat at the table. "Have you talked to his mom or dad anymore?"

"Not since last night. They're coming to the office this afternoon around three."

I mentally added the time to my day's schedule. The office, Scott's apartment, and the Sheriff's department. The sooner I started, the more info I could gather.

I hurried the kids along with breakfast then dropped Cole and Emma at school and Ivy at Doretha's. She'd babysat Cole and Emma and continued the tradition now with Ivy. She lived in a two-story, clapboard house dating back to the civil war. A mammoth structure, the house served as the parsonage for All Faith's Missionary Church and the area's local orphanage. Although not an orphan in the traditional sense, I was enough of one that Doretha took me in. To my knowledge, my birth mother still resided at the women's prison in Raleigh, serving a life term for shooting and killing my abusive father while he slept. Ivy had lost a parent to violence, too. We shared more than a signature on adoption papers.

I carried her into the homey kitchen where Doretha sat at the small table sipping her morning coffee. Chicory with milk, no sugar due to her diabetes. Ivy squirmed to play with Braxton, a four-year old with a mom in a methadone clinic and an unknown father.

"Good morning," Doretha said, sipping from her *World's Best Mom* mug. I had given it to her on my tenth birthday because she'd been such a gift to me. Twenty-five years later, the mug was faded, chipped even, but held together by sentiment.

I sat Ivy's diaper bag in the other chair. "Good morning."

"Coffee?"

My nose scrunched with no effort from me. Although the hazelnut smell of chicory was pleasant, memories of the bitter taste from childhood lingered. "Thanks, but I'll get a cup of real coffee at the office."

Doretha grunted. "Suit yourself. Any word on your delivery

boy?"

"The Swift Water Rescue is doing a grid search this morning. In one regard, I hope they don't find anything."

She stared into the mug, moving a spoon around in the froth. "And the other?"

Emotions hard to verbalize mingled with one another. "I suppose knowing is always better than the alternative."

Doretha sipped her coffee. "That's true. Much as it hurts sometimes. We prayed for him last night. Hope the good Lord sees fit to bring him home."

Praying for the best, expecting the worst. Sooner or later, the two collide and you're left numb to both. "I'll let you know if I hear anything."

I planted a kiss on the top of Ivy's head. Her blond hair, soft and clean, carried remnants of lavender baby wash. Occupied with her little friend, she paid me no mind. I liked it that way. Right after her mother died, she clung to me as if her life depended on it. In a way, I guess it did. I kissed her again out of my own need.

The *Jackson Creek Chronicle* operated in downtown Jackson Creek about two miles from Doretha out of an old mercantile store, complete with plank floors. Between me, a full-time reporter, a couple freelancers, an editor, an account exec, a graphic designer, and Nola, the office manager, we published a quality tabloid-sized newspaper every week. And up until last Thursday, Scott delivered it to ten thousand readers.

Nola was already at her desk, front and center. A widow in her mid-fifties, she worked because she didn't know how to not work. Her late husband's insurance policy paid for a red Mercedes and a Jamaican cruise once a year.

"I heard about Scott," she said as I passed, heading to my

desk. "Any word?"

News traveled fast in these hollers and hills, with or without a newspaper. Before I could answer, the phone rang and Nola spun around to grab it. "It's a great day at the *Jackson Creek Chronicle*. How may I help you?"

I dropped my bag at my desk then powered up the computer. Although my official office was in a converted storage room down the hall, I preferred to be out front with the rest of the staff in a low-key bullpen.

While the computer hummed to life, I grabbed a cup of coffee from the break room. Not much more than an over-sized storage room, the kitchenette held a small table with three mismatched chairs, a ten-year-old refrigerator, and a yard-sale microwave. Quinn Carter, my twenty-something investigative reporter, hovered over the brewing coffee. Hair unbrushed, clothes rumpled, red-eyed.

"Rough weekend?"

He grumbled something I didn't catch. "Heard anything on Scott?"

I leaned against the counter while we waited. "As of last night, no. They're resuming the search this morning."

When the brewing stopped, he filled his ASU mug with coffee strong enough to walk to his desk on its own. No sugar, no cream, no weak hearts. "You want me to open a file on it?"

The search for Scott Curry splashed across a headline delivered a punch to the gut I wasn't ready for. I wasn't sure how to answer. It *was* news worthy. Might even help. "Let me think on it."

Quinn raised a brow but apparently needed a caffeine fix before arguing with the boss. "Just keep me in the loop."

He started out, but I stopped him. "Hey, how well do you

know Scott?" I couldn't bring myself to speak in past tense.

Quinn lifted one shoulder. "We don't hang out or anything. He's still in school, right?"

"Yeah. A junior."

He slowly nodded. "I don't know that much about him. Sorry." After blowing into his coffee, he took a sip, then added, "He seems like a nice guy, though. Pretty clean cut so if...something happened, he was probably just in the wrong place at the wrong time."

The fact he didn't show for work plus the floating backpack was unsettling enough. The thought something other than an accident may have happened jarred me.

Quinn glared at me through skeptical eyes. "You have thought about that, right?"

Uncertainty spread across my face. Apparently, Quinn noticed. "Look, people like us—like me and Scott—we're not always welcome in these *hills and hollers*."

Maybe in the deep folds of my brain, that thought wiggled around a little, but not enough to wrangle its way into my conscious. I had suspicions but that's all they were. "Scott's gay?"

He blew into his coffee although I'm sure it had lost its heat. "I figured that's why you asked me how well I knew him."

I quickly shook my head. "No, not at all. I knew y'all were both in your twenties. And...." I stumbled over words buried somewhere between what we know to be right and wrong. "That wasn't the reason I asked you. At least I don't think it was."

Quinn laughed, cocked his head to the side. "Hey—it's okay. How long have we known each other? I know you're okay with it. With me."

Although Quinn was out with me, it wasn't public

knowledge. He was right about the hills and hollers. There were people who weren't as accepting as others. I often wondered what kept Quinn bound to this area rather than shooting for a network news position. He had the talent for a lot heavier news than ever happened in Jackson Creek, and the looks for the broadcast side of the profession. His sexual preference would be a non-issue in larger cities.

"I saw him at a club. He didn't see me," he said.

There was only one night club within fifty miles and I couldn't see the patrons being warm and friendly to a gay guy. "Around here?"

"Johnson City. It's underground. Kind of a *networking* thing."

"How long ago was this?"

He didn't have to think about it. "Last weekend. I didn't connect it to his no-show on Thursday until now."

"Did he leave with anyone?"

"I didn't see him leave so, I don't know." Another shrug.

Whether Scott left with someone or not, it didn't explain the backpack. Still, it was a start.

Nola popped her head into the break room. "Ava, the mayor's here to see you."

The microwave showed 8:12 in glowing green numbers. Justin Baker, the mayor of Jackson Creek, usually met us at the door. He was late.

"I'll be there in a minute." I finally got around to pouring a cup of coffee. Took a slow, long drink while wondering if Scott being gay did play into his disappearance. If so, I didn't want Quinn subjected to the closed minds that would come from interviewing potential witnesses. "Why don't you take the school renovation project and I'll take Scott. If there is a story there."

Fingers crossed, good thoughts, and prayers there wasn't.

Back out front, Quinn headed to his desk, and I headed to mine and the mayor. Justin Baker was a thirty-eight-year-old Ohio transplant with a gorgeous wife and two adorable kids who happened to get himself elected mayor on a whim. A decent guy who occasionally butted heads with the old establishment. If you, your parents, your grandparents, and great grandparents weren't born in these mountains, you were an outsider.

"Good morning, Justin."

Seated in the chair beside my desk, he leaned in as if to close the space between us, afraid what he was going to say could echo outside the office. "The Zoning Board's hearing a request this week on Mary McCarter."

"Mary? What kind of request is Mary making?" Mary and Keeper lived in a small, cluttered A-frame on the family farm off a dirt road in a holler barely in the town limits. It wasn't like Mary to request anything from anyone, especially the local government.

"Not Mary. Nancy Farmer."

Town Council member Nancy Farmer's roots in the area ran deeper than most of the trees so she made the town's well-being her mission in life. More often than not, her mission ended up being a major pain in my butt. "I'm not following."

He leaned back, settling into the cheap chair. "Nancy Farmer is requesting the zoning board look into Mary's, um, *practice*."

My blood pressure jumped a notch. "Why?"

Justin spread his hands, apologizing for his fellow council member's actions. A white-hot anger seared though my mind, stealing the words I wanted to spit out. Instead, I sat with my mouth agape.

Although Justin's warm eyes offered an apology, I wanted no part of it. He spread his hands again. "According to Nancy, what Mary is practicing is medicine without a license—"

"That's crazy."

From her desk in front of mine, Nola spun around in her seat. "Mary McCarter's been dispensing herbs and remedies for ages. No one's ever complained before."

Justin often earned my sympathy. Trying to keep the peace between busy-body adults who claimed to know the town's best interest was a never-ending saga. "Well, someone complained. And Nancy's vowed to look into it." A heavy sigh flowed slowly through his lips like air leaking from a tire.

Although I wouldn't put such an unfair request past Nancy Farmer, I didn't understand the motive behind this latest claim. Nancy balked at anything promising to bring the area into the twenty-first century. I'd figure she'd embrace granny witches and home remedies. "Where does Nancy get off saying Mary's practicing medicine?"

"Apparently, Mary gave one of her root remedies to Carlyle Hanson's son and he had a bad reaction to it."

The little dots running rampant in my brain started connecting. "And Carlyle's married to Nancy's cousin."

From his desk across the room, Quinn joined the conversation. "Well, as much as I hate to admit it, Nancy does have a point."

Justin scratched at his neck, a habit he resorted to when under pressure. Sometimes at council meetings, he'd scratch so hard he'd leave marks. "Technically—"

I jumped in before he had time to agree with Quinn. "Mary's a granny woman. That's what they do."

Quinn and Justin threw each other a look, Quinn's

complete with a smirk.

Nola brought out her best Southern drawl. "Y'all aren't from around here, are you?"

The truth was, I got where they were coming from. But both Quinn and Justin were outsiders, neither born and raised anywhere near Jackson Creek. They could live here the rest of their lives, raise generations of children here, but because their great-great grandparents settled nowhere near Jackson Creek, they'd never totally *get it*.

"So, what now?" I knew the process and Mary wasn't going to cooperate.

Justin squared his shoulders, more comfortable talking about municipal proceedings than mountain lore. "Nancy'll make a formal request at the next zoning meeting for the board to research it. If they find there's reason to proceed, they'll vote on it."

Mary McCarter was about as stubborn as they came. "You know Mary's not going to comply with whatever they come up with."

Justin slowly nodded. "Probably not. But she'll face some stiff fines if she doesn't."

"Oh come on, Justin. Mary doesn't have money like that. You and I both know it."

"Then she needs to comply. Maybe you can talk to her?"

If she didn't comply, the town would levy civil fines that she wouldn't be able to pay. If she didn't pay the fines and "fix" the problem, the town would be forced to take a lien on the property. Although everyone would know it was wrong, they'd be powerless to stop it. Not wanting to set a precedence, the town couldn't look the other way. I hated government.

Justin and I locked eyes, each knowing the situation wasn't

good. Although he held the title of Mayor, Justin Baker held little power. Especially with the Nancy Farmers of the world.

CHAPTER 5

After a second cup of coffee, I checked out of the office and took Hwy 321 toward Blowing Rock. Scott lived in a small complex with ten units, no pool or clubhouse, but a breath-taking view. Overlooking a lush green valley with a hazy, blue ridge backdrop, the view alone was worth the rent. A colorful star quilt displayed on the side of a barn brought the scene together like the perfect accessory to a comfortable home.

There were three cars in the parking lot, and none were Scott's. The ground unit of the first building sported a yard sign stuck in a tiny patch of grass indicating the resident manager's place. A bushy fern in a rope-like hanging basket swayed in a morning breeze while a well-used straw mat welcomed visitors.

The manager beat me to the door, opening it wide before I had the chance to knock. "Good morning – Frankie Reynolds, resident manager. Something I can help you with?" Still in a faded checked housecoat and bedroom scuffs, she offered her arthritic hand.

I shook her hand gently, afraid of hurting the curled fingers and swollen knuckles. "I'm Ava Logan. I'm checking on an employee who didn't show up for work. Scott Curry. I believe he lives in apartment Four-A."

Behind thick glasses, her eyes opened wide. "Oh! You're the newspaper lady. I love that little paper. Scott brings me one every Thursday." Her expression turned sour as her knobby hand moved to her lips. "Oh my. He didn't bring one last week. You don't think something's happened, do you?"

"I hope not. Do you think I could have a look around his apartment?"

Frankie nodded quickly. "Of course. Let me get the key." She returned a moment later still in her housecoat and slippers but with key in hand.

I followed her down the short walkway to Scott's apartment. The small patch of overgrown grass in front of each unit gave the place a disheveled look, like the apartments were on a twice-monthly mowing schedule regardless of how badly it needed it.

Frankie fought the limitations of her own hands while stabbing at the lock with the key. "He seems like a good boy, kinda quiet."

After watching her struggle, I offered to help. "Here, I'll get it." As soon as I opened the door, the cat Boone curled against my leg. The big tom meowed loudly. An overpowering smell of an unchanged litter box nearly made me gag.

Frankie covered her nose. "*Phew.* I told him he wasn't supposed to have pets."

I bent to stroke Boone's head, but the cat pulled away and darted into the small kitchen. I followed, noticing immediately the empty food bowl. Very little water stood in the other bowl. I poured him some dry food I found in a box under the kitchen sink.

Frankie clucked her tongue. "Poor thing acts like he ain't

eat in days."

The same dreadful thought wormed its way into my mind.

Scott's apartment sported college-kid-on-a-budget decor complete with yard sale furniture. The Shimano mountain bike propped in the corner cost way more than the threadbare sofa. Although school was out for the semester, a couple notepads and books lay scattered on a small dinette table. I thumbed through them, not sure what to look for. Maybe he'd enrolled in summer school? *A Pictorial Guide to Snakes of North Carolina, Wildflowers of Western North Carolina, The ABC's of Poison, From Mountain Lions to Black Bears* and *When New Age Religion Meets The Holy Spirit,* marked property of the Jackson County Public Library. Not Brighton College. So his interest was personal, not academic. Probably planning an extended hiking or camping trip.

Not finding anything useful, I moved to a stack of mail on the bar. Cable bill, cell phone bill—both opened and dated three weeks ago. A couple pieces of junk mail marked for resident.

Frankie peered over my shoulder. "Want me to go check his mailbox? There might be something in there?"

"Sure."

While she was outside, I went to his bedroom. Bed unmade, rumpled sheets, pillow case hanging half off a stained pillow. A discarded energy drink can in the trash, handful of loose change strewn about the dresser, the toe of a sock poking out of one of the drawers. Bike helmet and gloves in the floor alongside a cat carrier. I opened the double closet, wondering if his clothes were gone. Disappointed, but not surprised to see it full of jeans and shirts.

Frankie returned, clutching several envelopes. "I don't think he checked his mail very often. He's got a bunch here from lawyers, too, looks like. Think he was in some kind of trouble?"

I took them from her and thumbed through them myself. At least a dozen were from attorneys, all marked either "solicitation for representation" or "legal advertisement."

"Looks like he got a speeding ticket." I carried the letters back into the kitchen and started to stack them on the counter with the other mail but thought better of it. Most of these solicitations referenced a date and location of the ticket.

Frankie gasped as I tore into one. "That's against the law, messin' with someone's mail, it is."

"Yes. And that's why we won't tell anyone." I skimmed over the letter, searching for information. The date of the ticket was two weeks ago, issued in Virginia.

So it had been well over a week since Scott had checked his mail. Just as I stuffed the letter back into the envelope, a car door shut outside. Frankie hurried to the front window and peeped between the blinds. "It's the sheriff's department. I don't want no trouble." She turned, her face filled with concern.

"It's okay. You have every right to be here." I opened the door, not terribly surprised to see Detective Steve Sullivan, hands on hips, looking around the small complex like he needed a map.

What did surprise me was why Grayson sent Sullivan, a detective? A deputy could've handled a simple canvas and interview with the apartment manager.

With his mouth working a piece of candy from one side to the other, Sullivan lifted his sunglasses and glared in my direction. "Ava?"

"Steve. I guess you're here about Scott Curry?"

He moved the candy around in his mouth, buying time, any form of media his perceived enemy. "Yep. And I guess you're here doing my job."

I let the comment slide, more concerned with finding Scott than playing word games with a territorial detective. "Grid search turned up anything yet?"

He lowered his sunglasses and shook his head. "Nope."

Frankie pulled her housecoat tighter around her bony frame as she introduced herself. "I'm Frankie Reynolds, the property manager."

Joining us on the sidewalk, Steve flashed his gold shield. "Mind if I take a look at Mr. Curry's apartment?"

Frankie shook her head in a jerky fashion, rattled nerves getting the better of her. "No sir, not at all. Right this way."

Inside, the cat curled around my leg, emitting a loud meow. Although the tom provided at least one answer—it'd been days since the litter box had been emptied—he presented a problem. What to do with him? We couldn't lock him back up in the apartment with so many unanswered questions.

Sullivan scrunched his nose, his face bunching into a disgusted look. No doubt the overflowing litter box the culprit. "When's the last time you saw Mr. Curry?"

Frankie rubbed her hands, massaging her bent fingers. "Can't say for sure. Maybe one day last week. He didn't bring me my paper on Thursday, I know that."

Sullivan cut his eyes at me then continued looking around the apartment. "You don't remember the last time you saw him before that?"

"No sir. It wasn't anything unusual, though. Sometimes I wouldn't see him for days."

"He's a good tenant?"

"Oh, yes sir. Except for the cat." She waved a hand in front of her nose. "Paid his rent on time. No loud parties, or music, or anything like that. No problem whatsoever."

My phone chirped from my jeans pocket. I dug it out, surprised to see a text from Quinn. *Call me!*

I stepped outside and punched in Quinn's cell. He answered on the first ring. "What's up?"

"Some shit's going down at the McCarter's."

That grabbed my attention, pulling my eyes away from the view of the rolling ridges beyond the complex. "What kind of shit?"

"Apparently, someone from the zoning board showed up at the house and Mary and Keeper's not very happy about it."

At that moment, Sullivan bolted out of the apartment and rushed to his car. He cranked the engine, whipped the SUV around and sped off.

I looked back at Frankie standing in the doorway. "Steve Sullivan just got a call about something. I'll call Grayson and meet you at Mary's." I clicked the phone off and hurried over to the apartment.

"He got a call and tore out of here. I hope it wasn't about Scott"

"So do I." I pulled a business card from my phone case and handed it to Frankie. "If you hear anything, or think of anything, would you mind calling me?"

She shook her head. "Not at all. I hope nothing's happened to him."

"Me too."

I was already back at the Tahoe when Frankie called out, "What do I do about the cat?"

We did not need a cat. But I couldn't leave it.

I quickly gathered Boone's food and bowl, shoved him in the cat carrier then put it all, cat included, in the back of the

Tahoe. "You might want to just throw that litter box away."

Out of the parking lot, I took a deep breath to calm the nervous energy. The road curved sharply to the left, leaving the right side exposed to a steep drop off. With no guardrail, fear was the only barrier between making it to your destination or rolling down the side of a mountain.

Once I had a handle on the curves, I called Grayson "Sullivan just bolted from Scott's apartment. What's going on?"

"There's a disturbance over at the McCarter's."

At least Sullivan's frantic reaction wasn't related to Scott. "Yeah, Quinn called. I'm on my way over there."

"What are you doing at the apartment?" A slight twinge of attitude percolated in his voice.

I ignored it. "He has a cat. If it's been a few days since Scott's been home, I thought the cat might need food."

Boone meowed loud enough, it carried through the phone. "You have the cat with you?"

"I couldn't leave him there. Not knowing." *If Scott would be back* nearly rolled off my tongue. Guilt for abandoning my search of his apartment gnawed at me. I wanted to do more.

Grayson brought my attention back to the McCarters. "Hey, whatever's going down at Mary and Keeper's, stay out of the way, okay?"

My lips fought off a grin. We'd known each other over a decade and had been together a while. He still reminded me to be careful, knowing I'd more than likely ignore him. "Of course. But I do need to watch the road. Call me if you turn up anything on Scott."

I ended the call then gripped the wheel with both hands. The McCarter property sat in the bottom of a holler, surrounded by winding dirt roads snaking around a series of hills. The S-curves that narrowed to one lane brought a prayer that anything on the other side of the bend wasn't coming in my direction. If the ride wasn't so harrowing, one might enjoy the view of the blooming mountain laurel and patches of wildflowers scattered throughout the holler.

Around the last bend, Sullivan's department-issued SUV along with two other patrol cars and a State Trooper Crown Vic parked haphazardly in the McCarter yard, lights still flashing blue and red. An engine from the volunteer fire department sat off the road beside Quinn's Pathfinder. Quinn and the department captain sheltered behind the engine, waiting. Watching.

Mary McCarter stood in the doorway of her clapboard house, arm outstretched across the opening, Keeper behind his mother's protective barrier. Mary's other arm cradled a shotgun. Bob Palmer, with the county zoning department, perched one foot on the first step of the porch, both hands in the air. Sullivan and one of the uniformed deputies were positioned a few feet behind Palmer, the deputy's drawn gun leveled at Mary.

The reality of what I was seeing squeezed my lungs, stealing the air I needed. Rational thought or not, I jerked the Tahoe to a stop, barely shoving it into park before leaping out. "Jesus! What are y'all doing?"

Sullivan spun around as I barreled past him. He grabbed for my arm, missing. "Ava! You can't—"

I stood between Sullivan and Bob Palmer. "Mary, what are you doing? Put your hands down, Bob."

"He needs to get off our property," Keeper said from behind his mother.

Mary adjusted the shotgun, getting a better grip on the stock. "Ain't putting the gun away long as ones pointed at me and my boy."

I turned back to the deputy, corralling my anger that the dilemma had reached this point. "Can we deescalate this situation, please?"

Sullivan stomped up behind me. "Why don't you wait in the car. We've got this handled." He took my elbow, giving a slight tug in his direction.

I jerked my arm away, my anger boiling over. "No you don't have this handled, Steve. There's no reason for guns to be drawn. Tell your deputy to stand down."

"That boy charged at me," Bob Palmer stuttered, sweat rolling down his balding head.

Keeper bowed up behind his mother. Far from a boy, but people tended to forget that. "You come up here on our porch telling momma 'bout all these rules we gots to live by. Ain't sitting right."

I stepped past Bob, making my way up on the porch. "Keeper, no one's going to make you do anything. Let's sit down and talk it over, okay? I know you can do that."

Mary's fingers moved gingerly along the gun's stock, her stoic expression never wavering.

"Ava, you really need to let us handle this," Sullivan said from behind me.

"There is no *this*. It's over. Right, Mary? We're going to sit down—with Bob—and let him talk. We're going to have a glass of tea and maybe even laugh about this."

Sullivan sighed loud enough for everyone to hear, but Mary nodded to Keeper to move away from the door. She sat the gun beside the threshold then turned back inside the house.

From the porch, I glared at Sullivan. "*That's* how you handle the McCarters," I said, my voice a firm whisper.

“You know I could arrest you.”

I sliced him into tiny pieces with a cutting gaze then ushered Bob Palmer inside.

CHAPTER 6

Mary McCarter had graced the earth for close to seventy years. Never married, she'd bore the brunt of the gossip mill seemed like all her life. No one knew for sure who fathered Keeper, and that too, Mary kept private. Although living under the weight of an accidental pregnancy in a different era, she told me once she never considered giving the baby up for adoption or ending the pregnancy altogether. "He's a keeper," she'd said about her baby boy with the liquid brown eyes and simple mind.

Soft spoken and careful with her words, Mary lived a quiet life in the little house on the family farm in the holler. At least up until today. Faded, well-worn jeans hung on her narrow hips as Bob Palmer, Quinn, and I followed her into the small kitchen. The quick-draw deputy tagged along. Just in case. Mary's unencumbered silver-gray hair swept her back like a broom as she walked. Wiry and thick, it dominated her slender frame.

Known in these hills as a *granny woman*, or granny witch as they were sometimes called by the more dramatic, Mary had the gift. She had the knowledge of herbs and tonics and mystical ways that couldn't be explained. The tradition and culture of granny women dated back centuries in Appalachia. Some of the ways were borrowed from the Cherokee, others brought over by the Scots and Irish. Although rooted deep in Christianity, the traditions were often called witchcraft by outsiders to the mountains and those not knowing any better.

In the McCarter's kitchen, a stew pot boiled on the ancient stove, creating a glistening sheen of moisture on the yellow painted walls. A marred metal tea kettle rumbled from the foil-lined burner beside the pot. Grease-stained curtains fluttered in a breeze pushing through the open windows. Mason jars of varying size, each filled with plants or liquids, sat perched in the window sills and on the years-old Formica counter top. Aside from the smell of ginger boiling on the stove, the kitchen smelled dank and musty, like the land outside had seeped through the walls.

"Have a seat." Mary waved toward the worn maple table. Quinn bypassed the cane-back chairs and leaned against the counter instead, leaving the four chairs to myself, Bob, and the McCarters. Mary took five glasses from an open cupboard, four featuring the cartoon characters from The Flintstones and one from Scooby Doo, then filled them with her sweet tea. After she sat them on the table, Bob reached for the Scooby Doo glass, but Mary pulled it away, sliding one of the others over to him instead.

She slid the lone glass in front of Keeper. "My boy likes that one."

Keeper drank from the glass with purpose, eyes never moving away from Bob. I sipped from the Wilma Flintstone glass. The McCarter's sweet tea birthed a legend in these parts. Much like Mary's remedies, no one knew for sure what ingredients she used but no one ever complained Until now.

With the matter of Scott Curry still fresh on my mind, I wasn't sure why I felt so inclined to stay. Although Quinn didn't get the significance of granny women to these parts, he could easily cover the news angle, if there was one. After another sip, I wiped my lips and got down to business. "So why exactly are you here, Bob?"

He shot me a look, eyebrows raised. "Why are you?"

"Because I asked her to stay," Mary said.

But she hadn't. Unless my inclination to hang around was rooted in some weird form of the supernatural. I pushed those thoughts aside and took another sip, still feeling the sting of Bob's question. "Quinn's here as a reporter; I'm here as a friend. Mary's dear to a lot of people in these mountains."

"Not doubting it, Ava. Just doing my job." He blew a heavy breath through his nose, not happy the press was present but there was little he could do about it. "So there's been a request to look into these *tonics* and *remedies* Mary dispenses and see if there's a need for some kind of license." He flopped his hand back and forth at the mention of tonics and remedies.

"Momma's got license." Keeper jerked around to his mother. "Tell him, Momma. She keeps 'em in her billfold."

After handing a glass to Quinn, Mary finally sat, planting herself calmly beside her son. "Not that kind of license, Keeper."

I saw the confusion in his eyes. "This is a special license," I said softly.

Bob cleared his throat, ready to continue. "It's been brought to the zoning department's attention that some of these, um, *remedies*, can be considered medicinal."

"What's that mean, Ava?" Keeper looked from Bob to me, anxious for answers he wasn't going to like or understand.

Ignoring him, I turned to Bob. “Of course they’re medicinal. They’ve been that way for hundreds of years. Why is it an issue now.”

Mary slowly screwed the cap back on the Mason jar of tea. “Because someone didn’t follow directions.”

Bob spread open the folder he’d had tucked under his arm. “I’m not here to argue with you, Miss McCarter. I’m just here to gather some information about what exactly it is that you do.”

Mary’s expression never wavered, but mine did. “You know what she does, Bob. You were raised around here.”

Sweat rolled down his cheeks. The collar of his pull over shirt darkened from the moisture. Whether from the stifling heat in the cluttered kitchen or nerves from being on the wrong end of a shotgun, I didn’t know. I suspected a little of both. “I’m just doing my job, Ava.”

A small part of me understood that, but the part that didn’t was winning. There’d been many times I published an article because it was my job, not because I liked the content. “It’s no different than that Wonderworks Fat Burner stuff Gina Spivey sells.”

Mary arched a brow in defense. “*No*,” she said, the word creeping up her larynx, hanging on her tongue. “The difference is I don’t lie to people. Give ’em false hope. And I don’t sell the remedies. That’d be against the way of tradition.

I conceded. “Okay, bad example. But what I meant was all those wonder drugs that skirt by the FDA, people aren’t required to have a license to sell those.” I used air quotes around *wonder drugs*.

Keeper slammed his hand on the table. He rose up in his chair to challenge Bob, and me. “My momma don’t sell no drugs. You take that back.”

I quickly shook my head hoping to diffuse his hot anger. Hoping that shotgun was still in the living room and not in the kitchen. "Not that kind of drugs, Keeper. This is like...ginseng. You know how some people sell 'seng. That's all."

Everyone around here understood 'seng. Even simple-minded Keeper McCarter knew the real drug plaque seeping through these hills, and knew it wasn't good. Inner cities didn't have a lock on the drug epidemic. Meth, opioids, fentanyl—shattered lives regardless of the zip code.

Bob took a stout drink of his tea then pushed his empty glass toward Mary. He waggled thick fingers in her direction. "Despite what it looks like, I'm not the enemy."

While Mary filled Bob's glass with more of the drink, Keeper stared hard at the man, still angry. "Just cause you ain't the enemy don't mean you're our friend. Right, Momma?"

Such wisdom from someone deemed *simple*. Mary gathered her hair over her shoulder, working it into a tight braid, still without speaking.

Bob riffled through several pieces of paper bared in the open folder, finally settling on one. "What would you say is the number one ingredient in your remedies, Miss McCarter?"

"Belief."

The tea kettle blasted a shrill whistle, causing my insides to catch. Keeper jumped up and sat the kettle off the stove. "Water's done Momma. Want me to pour it?"

Mary had yet to look away from Bob. "Later, son."

Bob tilted his head toward Mary. "Another remedy?"

Mary's thin lips turned upward in a sad smile. A misunderstood smile. "Instant coffee. The *remedy's* boiling on the stove."

"And what would that be?"

"Ginger tea. Good for stomach ailments."

Bob jotted a note on his paper. "And you sell this out of your home?"

After tossing the perfect braid over her shoulder, Mary sat back in her seat. "I don't *sell* anything, Bob. Never have. Never will. I told you it was against tradition."

"And what tradition would that be?"

I huffed before Mary got the chance. "The tradition of granny women, Bob. Dates back centuries."

Mary stopped fiddling with her hair and leaned into the table, arms folded like she was testifying at a senate committee meeting. "Didn't your granddaddy's people come from 'round Linville?"

"They did."

Mary nodded. "Inis Woodrow delivered most of the babies back then in Linville. She probably delivered some of your folk."

No one said anything as we watched the standoff. Who would concede first in the stare down between the two?

Although Bob was supposed to be the one asking questions, Mary continued, "Wasn't it your daddy that got burnt real bad when he was a little boy? Pulled a pot of boiling water down on him, wasn't it?"

Bob sighed heavily. "I believe that's what happened."

"Inis Woodrow talked the fire out of his little arms and legs, if I remember the story right."

Defeated, Bob breathed deeply. "That's what I heard."

Mary poured him another round of tea. "Now, what was it you wanted to know about the granny woman tradition?"He shifted his weight in the chair. The cane back chairs lacked comfort and weren't intended for company to sit a spell. "It's not as much about the tradition as it is the remedies. There are ordinances that do require a license when you sell products."

Mary shrugged. "We don't sell them. I just give them away. Is there some kind of ordinance against that?"

If there wasn't one, Nancy Farmer would create one. "I don't think there's any kind of ordinance in the zoning books that even applies here. Is there?" I asked.

Bob finished off another round of tea then pushed his glass to the side. "Simple as it sounds," he said, "there's not an easy answer. There are ordinances that require a business license for certain types of businesses. Depending on the nature of the business, there may be zoning regulations that have to be met. Parking for instance–"

Mary cut him off. "Oh hogwash. With all y'alls cars out there, there's more vehicles here now than there's been in thirty years."

"That's right," Keeper said, poking his sharp chin out for emphasis.

Although I doubted he knew what he was agreeing with, regardless, I backed him up. "The fact the remedies aren't sold does make it hard to claim it's a business."

Mary waved her hand, shooing away the nonsense. "Ain't no business. It's a way of life in these parts. Simple as that."

"Simple as that," Keeper added. A solid shake of his head solidified his take on the subject.

Mary pushed her chair back and pulled herself up from the table. "If y'all excuse me, I need to get this tisane made before it turns bitter."

"I got the trots," Keeper said. "Momma's tea will fix me right up."

I struggled to contain a grin when Bob closed his folder. Over at the counter, Mary poured the mixture through a strainer into a mug in the aged stained, porcelain sink. Steam rose from the brew like fog lifting over the mountains. After adding a good heaping of honey, she placed the mug in front of Keeper then made herself a cup of instant coffee.

"Y'all like a cup?" She turned and leaned against the counter rather than re-joining us at the table, a gentle hint that all this zoning nonsense was over.

Bob stood, shaking his head. "Appreciate it but I think I'm done here. Going to head back and write up my report."

Bob gave me a curt nod, then offered his hand to Mary. "I'm sorry if this was unpleasant for you, Mary. Hopefully we can get it all straightened out real soon. I'll be back in touch if need be."

Mary made a sweep of the room with her hand. She motioned toward the front door. "Keeper, show our guests out, please. Got a busy day today. Ava, I'd like for you to stay a minute if you don't mind." I had a busy day, too. Getting sidetracked to the McCarter's wasn't on my schedule. Finding Scott was. Whatever the reason Mary wanted me to stay, needed to be a quick conversation. Quinn, the deputy, and Bob followed Keeper out of the kitchen and into the living room. The screen door popped against the frame followed by footsteps landing heavy on the wooden steps.

"He's not in the river," Mary said.

I jerked my head up, escaping my own thoughts, staring at her. "Pardon?"

"The boy you're looking for. He's not in the river."

CHAPTER 7

I sucked in a gulp of air, staring at Mary, frightened and bewildered. Brewing tonics and remedies weren't Mary McCarter's only gift. Rumors of other *abilities* had floated around town from time to time, quickly discarded by naysayers and amped up by teenagers hoping to scare their friends. The gift of insight only added to the mystery that surrounded her. "If he's not in the river, where is he?"

She shook her head, the braid swinging like a pendulum. "Not sure. The woods, maybe?"

I stepped over to her at the counter, my pulse quickening. I wanted to grab her bony shoulders and shake the answer out of her, shake out the answer I wanted to hear. "Is he alive?"

"I can't say for sure." Using a pair of small pruning snips, Mary trimmed back a stalk of rosemary. Although fragrant, the essence melded with the dankness overpowering the heated kitchen.

I pushed. "Do you see him?"

She moved on to a ginseng root. "No. Not anymore."

"What did you see when you saw him? Can you identify the location?"

She lay the snips on the counter then sipped from her coffee, slowly and deliberately. The coffee had to be cold by now but she drank it. She narrowed her eyes as if she were recalling something.

Although I wanted to shake the living crap out of her, I lightly touched her arm, reminding her gently a young man's life may be at stake. "Mary—"

"I was ten years old when your daddy was born. I went with my grandmother to your grandparents' house and watched her deliver him. Grandmother delivered a lot of babies in these mountains, but that one...I remember the look on her face when she was cleaning him up. That look people get when something's wrong. Kinda white-faced." She took another long drink of the coffee, the well-timed pause reminding me of my twisted lineage.

My patience grew thin with the drama. "My father's been dead close to thirty years. He has nothing to do with Scott Curry."

Mary sat her cup down. "Oh, but he does, Ava. There's a strong connection."

"Mary—"

"That's all I can tell you. I'm sorry there's not more." She took a well-used wicker basket down from a shelf, picked up the snips, then went out to the backyard.

Stunned, and aggravated, I pursued an answer, any answer. My heart thumped wildly as I hurried down the steps. I caught up to her at a garden bed. "There has to be more. Help me, Mary. Help me understand. *Please.*"

At a raised garden bed, she gently bent a cluster of lemon balm to its side and snipped near the bulb, then laid the leaves in the basket. Her lack of urgency tested my tongue as I swallowed a dictionary of expletives. "For the love of God, Mary—how is Scott Curry connected to my father?"

She jerked around and stared at me, shielding her eyes from the glaring sun with a leathery forearm. "Evil, Ava. Evil. That's the tie that binds them."

I had trusted Mary my whole life. Believing heart and soul in her abilities but this tested me in more ways than my tongue. Scott was one of the nicest guys I'd ever met. There was no way he could be connected to my father. My father had been Satan in the flesh. An abusive drunkard with a reputation that bordered legend in these hills.

Mary turned back to her herbs, clipping more lemon balm then adding it to her basket. "I'm sorry, Ava. I wish I could see more. Maybe in time I will."

And just like that, the discussion was over. Glancing past the garden and the old shed with Keeper's bicycle leaning against the rusted door, past the obsolete tobacco barn, to the mountains beyond the holler creeping upward into the hazy blue sky, I wondered what evil could grow out of something so serene.

There was no way to know what lay beneath the surface. Jackson Creek guarded its secrets like a mother bear protecting its cub. I slowly exhaled, resigning myself to accept the unanswered questions. The answers would come in due time.

I left the McCarter's and drove into town, anxious to meet Scott's family at the sheriff's office. The department was housed in the old Jackson Creek Bank & Trust, a three-story clapboard building with age-yellowed windows and an outdated ventilation system. When the air conditioning kicked on, lights in town flickered for a moment. The bank's three vaults had been turned into six-by-eight holding cells where the occasional prisoner stayed until transferred to Avery County.

The department's secretary, Annie Thompson, sat perched behind a green marble counter that at one time had been used by the bank's tellers. Annie was as old as the building itself. Although the department staff worked at the discretion of the sheriff, Annie came with the job. Her tenure was never questioned. It was understood.

With cat-eye glasses resting on her nose, she glanced up from her work as I entered. "Grayson's back in the interview room," she said, bobbing her head toward the hallway. "That boy's parents are with him."

I nodded and headed in the direction indicated. "Thanks, Annie."

"Um...Ava—you can't go in...." The sound of her voice faded as I moved out of earshot.

I paused at the door, steeling my nerves with a deep breath before opening it. *That's the tie that binds them,* I heard Mary say. Like a velvet whisper, tickling my mind. Except this wasn't pleasant. It was—*evil.*

I opened the door and saw Mr. And Mrs. Curry were seated at the long table, clutching one another's hands as if siphoning hope from one another. A girl I guessed to be early twenties sat next to the mother. Scott's sister, judging by the resemblance. Same high forehead, hooded hazel eyes, auburn hair.

A legal pad scribbled with notes in front of him, Grayson sat across the table from the family. He stared, his eyes unflinching, before standing and pointing to the door.

Grabbing the second before I'd be thrown out, I shoved my hand at Scott's father. "Mr. Curry, I'm Ava Logan, Scott's boss at the paper."

He stood, accepting my hand, the shake weak and timid.

"Ms. Logan. Scott's talked highly of you."

"Please, call me Ava."

Grayson pointed at the door more forcefully. "Ava, can I see you outside?" He didn't wait for me to answer. With his hand on the small of my back, he pushed me toward the hallway. "Excuse us just a minute."

He closed the door behind us then blocked it with his body.

"Scott's my employee."

"He's their son. You have no business in there."

"Grayson—"

"Ava." His Sinatra-blue eyes stared right through me, jaw set firm, breaths flowing slow and steady. Always cool under pressure. I always loved him but sometimes I hated him.

I shoved a lock of hair behind my ear then crossed my arms. "Look, Grayson—I want to talk to them, too. As Scott's *employer*."

"You're welcome to talk to them when I'm finished. Not now. I'll let them know you're waiting in the lobby."

"Grayson...."

He opened the door, started in but stopped and turned back to me. "Don't make this a headline, Ava," he whispered before disappearing inside the interview room.

My jaw fell slack at the comment. Rage bubbled to a boil as I grabbed the door knob, ready to set him straight. I slammed against the door, meeting resistance at the lock. How dare he! For the comment, and for locking me out.

Like a whipped puppy with my tail between my legs, I trudged back to the lobby. Annie glanced at me over her glasses. "Told you."

I plopped into one of the mis-matched yard sale chairs that made up the lobby. I didn't want to give in to defeat but Grayson wasn't playing. He'd throw me in jail if I pushed too hard. Our jobs got in the way of our relationship sometimes. If we were in a big city, we'd be adversaries. Here, we helped on another more than hindered.

"Sorry," Annie said from behind the marble desk. "He doesn't have an easy job."

I didn't acknowledge whether I agreed or not. No one had an easy job these days. Granted, some were tougher than others, but Grayson Ridge wasn't alone in that category. Didn't give him the right to be patronizing. I stewed a while longer then finally spoke. "I've never burned him, Annie. I've never published anything that could jeopardize an investigation. And he knows that. Besides, I *am* Scott's employer."

"Uh-huh," she mumbled before taking a call.

I sat there stewing for nearly an hour before Grayson and the Currys emerged from the interview room. Whatever anger I had evaporated when I saw Mrs. Curry's face. Red eyes, blotched cheeks, fear competing with shock. Not knowing what to say or do. Picking apart your son's life, clinging to a morsel of hope. I tried to imagine the emotions involved in being the parents of a missing child. Although Scott was a grown man, she was still his mother.

She clutched her daughter's arm with one hand for support. With the other, she dabbed at her eyes with a crumpled tissue.

Questioning them now seemed cruel.

Mr. Curry seemed to share the same thought. He hung back as his wife and daughter headed outside to their car. "I'm sorry. Maybe we can talk later this afternoon."

I dug a business card from my bag and handed it to him. "I understand."

He turned the card over and over in his hand, rubbing his

thumb over the embossed logo like it offered insight into his son. Maybe it did. "We're staying at the Valley Bed and Breakfast. Maybe you could join us for dinner. Around six?"

"I'll be there." Smiling politely, I asked his number then wrote it on the back of a separate card as he recited it.

I watched them drive away in their family sedan, safe, and typical. If one didn't know the drama enveloping the Curry family, you'd see them as pure Americana. Mom and dad, traveling in their older midnight blue four-door Chevy. A faded, peeling bumper sticker that once proudly proclaimed a son or daughter as an honor student. Was it Scott or his sister? Or both?

"I'm sorry you didn't get to talk to them," Grayson said, grabbing my attention away from the fading car.

My anger with him for his earlier remarks bubbled under my skin. But my empathy for the Currys was stronger. I pushed the anger out of mind. "I'm meeting them later. Anything you can tell me from your meeting?"

We headed back to his office. "They're not sure the last time they talked to him, they don't know his schedule. Not unusual, really. So what exactly happened at the McCarters?" The tone of his voice was hard to gauge. No telling what Steve Sullivan had reported back.

"Bob Palmer went over to Mary's thinking he was going to actually get somewhere with a zoning board request. Only thing he got was a shotgun pointed at him. You need to do something about your quick draw deputy before he gets someone hurt."

He closed his office door then pulled me to him, landing soft kisses on my neck. "Mary pulled on him," he mumbled through nibbles.

I moaned, tilting my head to give him access. The air was

hot; the old office stuffy. "And I told her to put it down, and she did. Problem solved. No headline there."

He pulled back, glaring through me. "Yeah...sorry about the comment."

"It was uncalled for. You know I'm more concerned about Scott than a headline."

He slowly nodded, lips pursed like he was contemplating his response. "You handle your end, and I'll handle mine. Deal?"

I landed a kiss firmly on his mouth, my tongue searching for his. My hands rested on his thighs, kneading the tight muscles with my fingertips. His breath hitched, catching in his throat. "See you tonight," I whispered and pulled away, my anger now only slightly smoldering.

CHAPTER 8

At home, I threw a frozen pizza in the oven for Cole and Emma while stepping over Finn, again and again. I was scheduled to meet the Currys for dinner at six and Finn's penchant for being at my feet was hampering the time line.

Emma was at the table pretending to study on her iPad. I hoped she wasn't looking at water-bloated bodies again. "I still don't understand why you left Ivy at Doretha's. I'm perfectly capable of babysitting."

"I know you are. But I don't know how long I'll be."

I caught a glance in my direction, a hitch in her breath. A flash of apprehension in her eyes.

Although we'd moved past the events of last fall when someone took a shot at me through the sunroom windows, the memory reared its ugly head on occasion. Sometimes I hated the world for robbing kids of their innocence. Especially my kids. I stepped over Finn and walked to my daughter, kissing her on the head. "I'll try and be home before dark."

She nodded slightly, turning back to her iPad. "If something...you know...bad happened to Scott are we goin' to keep his cat?"

The mind of a twelve-year-old never ceased to amaze me. One moment, terrified to be without an adult in the house after dark. The next looking at bloated bodies and wondering what's to come of a missing person's cat. "Hopefully Scott will be home in a few days and he can reclaim Boone. How's that?"

She shrugged. "I wouldn't mind keeping him. I mean if we had to."

"Well, he's fine in the laundry room for the time being. I'm not sure how Finn will react." And besides, I really didn't want a cat.

Cole bounded into the kitchen signing a song, fresh from a shower, hair wet and smelling like a walking commercial for AXE body spray.

I looked at the clock to double check the time. He never showered before dinner. "So, you going to tell me what's going on?" I asked.

He stared at me as if he didn't understand the question. "What do you mean?"

"The shower. The good mood. You're singing." I fluttered my hand in his direction as if to clarify whom I was talking about.

He grabbed a handful of grapes from the fruit bowl on the counter, popping them one by one in his mouth. "Oh yeah, I forgot to tell you. Paisley's coming over."

I could have sworn he said his sixteen-year-old girlfriend was coming over. "Excuse me?"

His mouth stopped mid-chew as the realization his mother wasn't happy with his forgetfulness sank in. "Um...it is okay, right?"

I jammed my arms across my chest and leaned against the

counter. "No, Cole, it's not. I'm not going to be here."

"Where are you going?"

"I'm meeting Scott's parents for dinner. You need to call Paisley and tell her another time."

The order was met with a sigh heavy enough to blow up a balloon. "Mom...*come on.* I didn't get to see her Saturday 'cause of that whole mess—"

"Did you see her today at school?"

"Well, yeah...but I mean, that was school."

My point exactly. "So what's the difference between seeing her at school and seeing her in your home?"

The wires in my son's brain short circuited as his mouth scrambled for an answer that wasn't there. Finally, his shoulders sank with an audible huff. "Oh come on, Mom. We won't do anything. You can even leave Brat here to rat us out."

Emma jerked her head up. "Hey!"

"We'll stay in the sun room. Brat can stay in there with us the whole time." He had slipped into full on pleading mode now.

Emma scrunched her nose. "Eww. No thanks."

The oven timer dinged, buying me another minute to consider the situation. I didn't want Emma to have to play chaperone. She would certainly tell me everything that went on, but it would be after the *everything* had already happened that worried me. "Cole, I'm sure her parents would have mixed feelings about it, too, so the answer is still no. Call her and invite her to come over tomorrow evening. I'll make certain I'm here."

Anger reddened his face as he stomped off upstairs, his bare feet slapping against the hardwood steps.

I turned back to the pizza and attacked it with a cutter. "So what do you know about this *Paisley*?" I asked Emma.

"She's really pretty. Long, curly blond hair. And she wears

some of the neatest clothes."

Not exactly what I was looking for, but should I really expect different from an almost teen? I fixed Emma a plate and carried it over to the table. After setting it down, I kissed the top of her head. "I'll have my phone on if you need me."

I pulled into the gravel parking lot of the Valley Bed and Breakfast, parking beside the Curry's sedan. The B&B sat tucked into the Big Blue Valley, so named for the surrounding Blue Ridge peaks. The deep purple blooms of wild indigo popped against the white mountain laurel framing the turn-of-the-century farm house. New owners with deep pockets renovated the place a few years ago, adding a green tin roof and front porch rockers.

Georgia Todd, the owner, greeted me at the front door with a tentative smile. "Mr. Curry told me you'd be joining them for dinner. I wish it was under happier circumstances."

"I do, too." I stepped inside, taking in the smell of cooking apples. Georgia, along with her husband Cal, moved to the area by way of Rhode Island. They were nice, pleasant folks who avoided the drama of small-town politics.

"I believe they're in the sitting room if you want to follow me. Dinner will be ready soon."

I followed Georgia down the long hallway, taking in the framed artwork lining the walls. Most were originals from local artists. I wondered if one had been painted by Ivy's birth mother, Trish Givens? Funny how a simple reminder of another Jackson Creek tragedy jerked me back to the here and now. I prayed this one had a happier ending.

Georgia ushered me into a comfortable back room filled

with overstuffed sofas and plush chairs, a regulation-sized pool table, and a stone fireplace stretching across the back wall. A wet bar sat tucked into an opposite corner.

Mr. Curry stood as I entered and offered his hand. "Miss Logan, thank you for joining us."

"Please, call me Ava." I shook his hand, unnerved by the quietness in the room. A wall-mounted television flickered the evening news with the sound muted. If I hadn't known better, I'd have sworn I was at a wake. Maybe I was.

Mr. Curry waved a hand at Scott's mother and sister. "This is my wife, Lisa, and our daughter Sara. And my name is Will."

Lisa appeared more composed than earlier in Grayson's office, yet her demeanor was still eclipsed with a noticeable sadness. Crows feet extended beyond the corners of her eyes and spread out toward her hairline. Like thin fingers holding her face together, holding herself together. But it was Sara that drew my full attention as her eyes met mine–intense, almost fearful.

Will pulled my gaze away as he motioned toward one of the overstuffed chairs. "Please, Ava, have a seat. Maybe you'll be able to shed some light on the situation."

"I was hoping the same of you." I offered a tentative smile. After settling into the chair, I took my notepad from my bag. "Do you mind if I take notes?"

"No, of course not. Anything that can help."

Sara watched me flip the pad to a clean sheet then turned away while picking nervously at a barely-there nail. Her mother Lisa moved to the edge of the sofa and clasped her hands together as if readying herself to pray. Instead she spoke in a soft voice. "You probably know more about Scott's day-to-day activities than we do. Is there anything that stands out recently?"

I wanted so bad to tell her yes, that he'd been acting odd. That he'd not been himself. Instead, I offered the only thing I had. "He just didn't show up for work last Thursday. That was the first indication something was off."

Will sat beside his wife, covering her hand with his. The simple gold wedding bands rested against one another. "Did you ever talk to him during the week? Maybe to confirm details?"

I slowly shook my head. "There was never any need to. He'd always call or send me a text if he was running late. But that hardly ever happened."

A tiny smile crept over Lisa's lips. "At least he texted you."

Will patted her hand. "He's just enjoying his independence. That's what college kids are supposed to do."

Sara pushed out of her chair, sucking in a deep breath. "I'm going to check on supper."

Will and Lisa acted oblivious to their daughter's abrupt departure. They may not have picked up on it but I did.

"So, Will, Lisa—when was the last time you talked to Scott?"

Lisa answered first. "For me it was about three weeks ago. He called wanting to know the name of a vacation cabin we used to stay at when he and Sara were kids."

"Was he planning a vacation?" With school out, it did make sense.

"Just a long weekend get-away, I think," Lisa said.

"Do you know when he was planning on going?"

She shook her head. "He didn't really say."

"What was the name of the cabin?"

"Bear Creek. It's rented through Dalton Realty." I wrote the name then asked, "Is that in North Carolina or Tennessee?"

"North Carolina. In Avery County."

"You don't know if he made reservations?"

She shook her head again and Will piped in. "We told the sheriff. He said he'd look into it."

It could turn out to be a good lead, or at this point, I'd take a good starting point. "Will, when was the last time you spoke with him?"

"The same. I talked to him for a few minutes after Lisa spoke with him. Just chit chat."

"Did he have any friends at school that you know of? Did he ever mention anyone?"

They looked at one another then each shrugged. "Not really," Will said.

Sara poked her head in the room and announced supper was ready. Her expression held nothing, no hope, no joy, no disdain. Not even a gleeful hint that we were about to eat a home-cooked meal. The lack of any kind of semblance of mood was baffling.

The three of us trailed Sara into the antique-filled dining room where Georgia had set out dinner. Family-style bowls of seasoned cabbage, mashed sweet potatoes, and stemmed apples made my mouth water. A slow cooked pork roast topped off the display.

In a sweet gesture, Will held the chair for his wife. I purposely sat across from Sara to keep her in full view. When our eyes met, she quickly looked away.

Georgia buzzed around the table like a busy bee. "I've got a buttermilk pie cooling so y'all save room for dessert."

"Sounds delicious," Will said as he took his seat beside Lisa. He was trying so hard to be upbeat despite the situation. It made me wonder if he was always so supportive or if he just recognized a need for comfort during a tough time.

After filling my plate, I forced a conversation with Scott's sister. “Sara, are you and Scott close?”

The suddenness of her inclusion startled her. She stared at me through wide, empty eyes then hurriedly filled her plate.

“Oh they’re very close,” Will said, speaking for his daughter.

She turned her eyes up, glancing at me, but didn’t respond.

“Are y’all close in age?” I asked, directing the question to her rather than her father.

But it was Will who answered. Again. “Two years apart. This has been hard on Sara. She’s always been the protector. Isn’t that right, sweetheart?” He waited for Sara to respond.

We all waited for Sara to respond. Finally, she offered a tiny nod. “But I couldn’t protect him this time.”

Lisa dropped her fork against the plate, the *clang* loud and startling. “Sara—don’t talk like that. There was nothing to protect him from. Scott’s fine. He’ll call any day now.”

Will shot me a glance then reached for his wife’s hand, lovingly stroking away the reality of their son’s disappearance. “That’s right. I’m sure he’s probably at the beach with some of his friends. Just forgot to tell us. That’s all.”

I wished that was the case but knew it probably wasn’t. “When’s the last time you talked to him, Sara?”

She lifted her shoulders in a casual shrug. “A few days ago, I guess.”

“We told the sheriff,” Will added.

Will Curry’s calm and supportive nature was growing into an issue. I wondered if the women of the Curry family were allowed to speak for themselves at home?

I tried again, fixing my eyes on Sara. “Do you know if Scott was planning on going away?”

“No,” she snapped, then jerked her eyes toward her parents, then quickly back to her food. “I mean, he didn’t say.”

"I'm sure he would have told us," Lisa said. "He wasn't one to keep secrets."

CHAPTER 9

After supper, Will answered a few more questions while Lisa battled an oncoming migraine. Sarah escaped to the front porch, away from the questions. After helping Lisa upstairs to lie down, Will returned to the sitting room and apologized. "I'm sorry. This has been so stressful on her."

"I'm sure. I can only imagine what you're going through."

He sat across from me, elbows propped on his knees, thumb and index finger rubbing at a callus on the other hand. "Scott's a good kid. Or man, I should say. This isn't like him at all."

Mary McCarter and her vision hammered away in my mind. *Evil. That's the tie that binds them,* I heard her say, again and again.

Will blew a tired breath, his shoulders giving way to the weight he carried. "I've just got that feeling, you know. Something bad's happened."

I pushed Mary's words to the far part of my brain. "You can't think that, Will. You have to keep the faith."

He continued rubbing the callused hand, probably unaware he was even doing it. "If you weren't his employer, would you be here?"

I frowned, my brows furrowed. "I'm not sure what you mean."

"Forget you're Scott's employer. Would you be here as a newspaper publisher?" He looked up, meeting my eyes.

A knot formed in the pit of my stomach. I was glad Lisa was upstairs. "If you're asking me if I think there's a story here, I can't answer that, Will."

"Can't or won't?"

"I don't want to think something bad has happened. But as the publisher of the town's only source of news, I have to consider all the scenarios."

He pulled himself up with more effort than his lean frame required, then walked to the picture window framing a distant blue-capped peak. "The public has a right to know, right?"

"Not always."

Judging by his reaction, my answer surprised him. He jerked around, hands in the pockets of his jeans and scrutinized me. "You're not a free press supporter?"

"Of course I am. But there are things the public doesn't always need to know."

"Where do you draw the line?"

What is it he doesn't want me to write? "It's a gray area, Will. I try to respect privacy, but, if public safety is at stake...."

He held his hand up, nodding. "I get it."

I stood, taking a step closer to him. Brick by brick, there was a wall forming and we were on opposite sides. "I'd never write anything to hurt Scott."

He nodded but didn't say anything. Finally, after a long moment, he said, "I need to go check on Lisa."

"How long are y'all planning on staying in Jackson Creek?"

"We're leaving tomorrow. We both have jobs we can't...." Every ounce of strength he'd shown in front of his wife, slowly slipped away.

"Will, I'm going to keep looking, I promise. I care about him, too."

He slowly nodded again then hurried up the stairs. I gathered my bag, hoping Sara would still be on the front porch. Outside, relieved to see her in one of the rocking chairs, I sat down beside her in the other.

"It's a beautiful view isn't it?" I said, looking out at the mountains beyond the valley. Dusk had washed the land in multi shades of pink while cicadas chirped in the distance.

She didn't say anything. Just kept rocking, slow and steady.

"Sara—"

"My brother's gay. My mom and dad don't know," she said, her voice faint. Afraid someone other than me would hear.

I looked out over the valley, at the peacefulness. The weight of camouflage burdened my soul. Whether the landscape or a person, nothing was ever what it seemed.

"Let's take a walk." I looked back over my shoulder at the screen door, hoping Will would stay occupied just a few more minutes.

Sara rose then followed me down the steps. I wasn't sure where we were going but it would have to be free from her father if I wanted her to open up. When we were far enough to ensure privacy, I slowed the pace. "Tell me about the Scott no one knows."

She pushed her hands into the back pockets of her shorts, hesitating before answering as if gathering her thoughts. "He was seeing someone. A guy named Josh."

"Do you have a last name?"

Shaking her head, she stopped walking. "I don't know his name, but I have his picture. Scott sent me a selfie with him."

She took her phone from her back pocket and scrolled through text messages. A thumbnail picture of Scott popped up in the left-hand corner. The contact named read "Bro." Sara opened the message link and stared at the little bubble of words she'd shared with her brother. OMGs, LOLs, emojis for every emotion – so little had been said but were now priceless conversations. She thumbed up until she came to a photo. She tapped on it to increase the size. The image was a selfie, taken from Scott's outstretched arm of himself and another guy. Could have been two pals on game day. The other guy was blond, blue-eyed. An awkward smile.

"Can you send me that picture?" I said and shared my contact information. A moment later, my own phone dinged, indicating a new message.

"Mom and dad can't know about Josh. When the sheriff asked if Scott was seeing anyone...and I couldn't tell him."

"Sara, your parents just want him home safe. I'm sure who he's dating isn't the issue."

A bitter laugh escaped her lips. "You don't know my dad."

Will's acceptance, or lack of, his son's lifestyle wasn't my main concern at the moment. "What do you know about Josh?"

"They met at school last fall and really hit it off."

"Did you ever meet him?"

She shook her head. "I wanted to, but we weren't ever able to work it out. With my work schedule and their school schedule, it was hard to get together."

We followed a worn path toward an old barn. A rusted plow lay on its side in a swath of grass, deserted and forgotten. A rabbit jutted from the shadow of the dull blade and disappeared into a patch of underbrush.

"Scott didn't come home on the weekends?"

She huffed a slight laugh. "Scott avoided home when he could. And Josh...I think he lived in the dorms and went home on the weekends."

I thought of what Quinn had said about seeing Scott in the bar but didn't mention it. "Were Scott and Josh exclusive?"

She shrugged. "I don't know. I mean, I don't know that Scott was seeing anyone else, but I could be wrong. He never mentioned anyone else."

We reached the shell of a barn, a stark reminder of a life forgotten. Simpler times. When good was good and bad was bad. What kind of fear raced through a child's mind with every creek of a board, every rustle of hay, every darkening shadow, like now with dusk falling? The *evil* that lurked in every corner was too often very real.

I didn't want to cut this short, but the encroaching darkness reminded me I had told Emma I'd be home by nightfall. "What else can you tell me about Josh?"

"I think Scott said he worked in the college bookstore, or maybe in the cafeteria."

"That's good. That's very helpful." I looked out over the darkened field as an owl hooted in the distance. "And what about Scott? Is there anything else your mom and dad may not know? Drugs? Alcohol?"

Sara quickly shook her head. "He's too much of a health nut. At least, I think he is."

That matched the Scott I knew. "What about social media? Facebook, Snapchat? Any of those?"

Hoping to beat the darkness, we started back to the house. "He's pretty private. If he's on any of those sites, I don't know about it. Please don't print anything about what I told you. Mom and dad don't need the added stress."

"Sara, Scott's sexual preference doesn't define him. It's no more important than the color of his eyes."

"I wish everyone felt that way. Mom and dad sure don't. Especially dad."

I hesitated before saying anything. I didn't know Will Curry enough to pass any kind of judgment. Instead, I offered the one thing I hoped to be true. "I'm sure they just want Scott home safely, regardless."

I left the Valley Bed & Breakfast and called Doretha from the road. "I'm sorry I'm running so late but I'm on the way."

She paused before answering. A lot of thought usually went into her silence. "Why don't you just leave her. She's already asleep anyway."

And just like that, no matter what I'd accomplished in the day, no matter the good, guilt smacked me square in the face. I'd taken on the responsibility of a toddler when I signed my name on her adoption papers. Not only that, it was well past dark and Emma would be wracked with worry.

Leaving Ivy with Doretha and going straight home would save me thirty minutes. Still, Ivy needed the stability of sleeping in her own bed, of having breakfast with her family. I'd make it up to Emma somehow. "Thanks for offering, but I'll come get her."

I hung up and called the house. Emma answered on the second ring. "You said you'd be home before dark," she snipped.

"I know. I'm sorry, honey, but I'm on my way. I'm going to pick up Ivy then I'll be home."

"Finn's been barking."

Emotion clutched at my heart, shooting a burning sensation through my chest. I'd never get passed the anger I carried for the shooter who violated my home, my kids' home and their piece of mind. "Close the blinds in the sun room. She probably sees a squirrel. Or she might just be hearing the river. Where's Cole?"

"In his room."

"Go tell—" I stopped mid-sentence. It wasn't her job to fuss at her older brother for me. She did enough of that on her own. "I'll call him. I'll be home in just a few minutes."

The signal cut out before I could say goodbye, which added to my stress and her fear. I'd call Cole when I got to Doretha's. Being in the middle of town, getting a cell signal was never a problem for the old house.

When I pulled up in the driveway, I tried Cole's cell phone. After five rings, it went to voicemail. I sent him a text message. *Go downstairs with your sister. Now. Reply.*

A moment later, my phone showed the message as delivered but not read. The porch light over Doretha's front door flickered to life. My anger with my son growing, I dropped my phone into the cup holder then went to retrieve Ivy.

Doretha met me at the door, holding it open with a finger pressed against her lips. "Shhh. Finally got everyone down," she whispered.

Every bed in every bedroom full of kids no one wanted, or whose grandparents just couldn't take care of while their meth-addict moms and dads spent their days in oblivion.

"I'm so sorry. I didn't think it would take this long."

She waved me off then tied her tattered housecoat a little tighter. "Did you find out anything from his parents?"

"Not much but it wasn't a wasted trip." I followed her into the den where Doretha had a portable crib set up for Ivy. She looked like such an angel, sleeping soundly, blond hair all mussed up. I hated to wake her but couldn't bring myself to leave her.

She stirred slightly as I lifted her but snuggled into my neck with her chubby arms wrapped tightly around her safety net. Doretha draped Ivy's bag over my shoulder then covered her with a lightweight blanket. The child's hair was already damp with sweat, but I left the covering in place. At least until I got to the car.

My arms ached by time I got to the Tahoe and buckled Ivy into the car seat. I had been in so much better shape when Cole and Emma were toddlers. Now I swore twenty pounds of dead weight could anchor a cruise ship.

I checked my phone again. No reply from Cole. But Grayson had called. *Crap.* He was supposed to come over. I punched in his number.

He sounded sleepy. "Hey—everything okay?"

"I'm so sorry. I got tied up with the Currys."

"How'd it go?"

I debated telling him what Sara had told me. Would he be under some type of ethical obligation to tell Scott's parents? "It went fine. Typical all-American family." That part wasn't a lie. "Hey, I'm really sorry it's so late. I guess I just lost track of time."

"Don't worry about it. Maybe we can make it tomorrow night. Go home and get some sleep."

I told him goodnight before my hormones got the better of me.

CHAPTER 10

The next morning, I rushed the kids along for school amid grumbles and muffled complaints. Sweet Ivy threw a tantrum over a crumbled Pop Tart and Emma didn't even try to console her. She was usually quick to play momma or at least the caring big sister. Apparently, it wasn't on today's agenda.

I glanced at the clock when Cole poured himself another bowl of cereal. "Ya'll need to hurry it up or we're going to be late."

"You mean *you're* going to be late," my son mumbled between bites.

"Excuse me?" I was not in the mood for a smart mouth or attitude this morning. Or any morning of late.

"Nothing."

"And oh, next time you don't reply to one of my texts, you can kiss your phone goodbye for a week."

He rolled his eyes then shoveled another spoonful of cereal into his mouth. I stepped over Finn and her new friend Boone and rinsed my coffee cup at the sink. I gave the kids another ten minutes then called breakfast as officially over. Dishes piled into the sink, I hefted a kicking and screaming Ivy from the high chair, wiped crumbs from her mouth with my fingers and headed out the door.

Later, with the kids deposited where they needed to be, I headed to Brighton College in search of Josh. Even with the semester over, the bookstore should still be open. I had my doubts about the cafeteria but maybe someone in the office would know a *Josh*.

The college sat on the Blue Ridge Parkway in a compact campus near Blowing Rock. A private college, I'd never questioned how Scott afforded it until last night when I met his parents. A scholarship, perhaps?

Old multi-story buildings with white columns stood in circular formation around an ancient oak tree. Benches surrounded a fountain leading into the main building. White rhododendron rushed to bloom early alongside the pink mountain laurel spotting the manicured grounds. I followed the driveway around to the back of the main building and searched for an empty spot. With school being out for the summer, the number of cars surprised me. All the more people to question.

The main building smelled of pine cleaner and air freshener embedded in the painted walls. My shoes squeaked against the spit-shined wood flooring. A glass case displaying sports trophies and plaques stretched the length of the main hallway. Oil portraits of past deans hung above the encased achievements.

A girl wearing a Brighton College t-shirt bounced out of the Registrar's office with too much energy for the time of morning. She glanced at me briefly before heading down a separate hallway. I hurried to catch up to her. "Excuse me—I'm looking for the book store," I said, taking her by surprise.

She pushed her lip ring out with her tongue and furrowed

her brow. "Oh, yeah. Um, it's in the annex building. You're in the main building."

I looked around the hallway, trying to figure out where the annex building was located. "And that would be...which direction?"

She looked me over then sighed and apparently decided I wasn't a threat. "Come on, I'll walk with you. It's kinda hard to explain. I used to work in the bookstore until I transferred to the office."

"Thank you," I said as we continued down the deserted hallway. "My name's Ava Logan."

"Josie Tortelli. It's nice to meet you."

At the end of the hallway, she pushed open a heavy double door leading to the outside. A concrete walkway snaked around the back of the building and under an aluminum awning.

"Does the book store work a full staff during summer?"

"That I don't know. I worked there during the school year. "

"What about the cafeteria? Is it open during the summer?"

Josie glanced sideways at me, her lip ring poking out beneath her pucker. "Are you some kind of inspector or something?"

I reached in my bag and pulled out a business card. Handing it to her, I said, "I'm with the *Jackson Creek Chronicle*. I'm looking into a student's possible disappearance."

We stopped walking as she turned the card over in her hand. "No kidding? Really? Who's the student?"

"Scott Curry. He delivers the paper and didn't show for work last week."

She stared at the card as concern spread across her face. She then slipped the card into the back pocket of her jeans. "Scott's missing?"

"Do you know him?"

"Yeah, he was in my poly-sci class. He's a real nice guy."

We resumed our walk to the bookstore, walking a little slower, perhaps more thoughtful. "How well do you know him?"

Giving it some thought, she shrugged. "Just kinda casually, I guess. I mean we didn't hang out or anything but would always chat when we saw each other. Man, I hope nothing's happened to him."

"Do you know who he does hang out with?"

"No. He lives off campus so he's not really into the dorm scene."

"What about a guy named Josh. He may work in the bookstore."

"It would have to be Josh Bloom."

I committed the name Josh *Bloom* to memory. "I had heard he's a friend of Scott's."

"Yeah." She didn't offer anything else and I didn't push. Not yet.

The walkway ended at a single-story brick building, longer than it was wide. With rooms on either side of a darkened hallway, it reminded me of the catacombs rather than a college. One lone light shone from a room at the opposite end.

Josie pointed down the hallway. "Where that light is—that's the bookstore. I'd walk with you, but I've got to get back to the office."

"Thank you so much, Josie. You've been a big help. If you hear anything about Scott, please give me a call."

"Yeah, sure. I hope nothing's happened. He really is a good guy."

I offered a tentative smile, hoping the same but having my doubts.

The bookstore occupied three adjoining classrooms with shelving, racks, and a register. The gold shag carpet and lack of a coffee counter transported it back to another decade. An older woman looked up from one of the shelves but didn't offer a smile.

"Can I help you?"

"I'm looking for Josh Bloom? I was told he works in the bookstore."

She continued straightening a line of books on the shelf. "He does. He'll be back the week after July fourth."

That long? "You wouldn't have a home address, would you?"

She glared at me over the top of her glasses. "No. I wouldn't. And I wouldn't give it to you if I had it. There's a thing called privacy."

I swallowed the barbs my tongue wanted to unleash. She'd already said she didn't know his address, so no amount of sarcasm would produce it. "Thank you," I said and smiled as warmly as I could despite wanting to chew her up and spit her out.

Although there wasn't an excuse for her rudeness, being stuck in a tomb all day would take its toll on me, too. As a private college, you'd think they'd allow more funding for the book store. Liven it up a little.

I retraced my steps down the hallway and headed back to the main building. Outside the annex building, I tried to search the Internet for *Joshua Bloom* but couldn't get a signal and the Wifi was secured. Maybe Josie could slip me the address?

After a wrong turn, I found my way back. The registrar's office buzzed with chatter from the few people at desks. Scott's name was mentioned followed by a noticeable hush as all eyes turned to me.

Josie nervously flicked her lip ring up and down. “I was just telling them about Scott. I hope that’s okay?”

“Certainly. Maybe one of you can help me track down one of his friends?”

“Josh wasn’t in the bookstore?” Josie moved behind one of the desks then powered up a computer.

As I joined Josie at her desk, another lady walked over. Not as old as the lady in the bookstore, she didn’t appear as grumpy, either. “What’s the friend’s name?”

Instinctively, I handed her a business card. “His name’s Joshua Bloom.”

“Oh, Josh.” She looked over my card, then added, “I love the *Chronicle*. Y’all do a great job with it. I’m Karen Ackerman. It’s nice to meet you.”

I accepted the compliment with a smile but was more interested in Josh Bloom at the moment. “Nice to meet you, too. So you know Josh?”

She pointed something out on the monitor to Josie. “Yeah, he’s...polite.”

Whether intended or not, the hesitation in her voice raised a flag. A big flag.

“I really need to get in touch with him. He’s good friends with Scott and—”

“Josh Bloom?” The woman furrowed her manicured brows to the extreme. “Are you sure about that?”

My thoughts collided with one another as I debated how to answer. Going on what Sara had told me, Scott and Josh were more than friends but that was no one’s business but their own. “Scott had mentioned Josh a few times,” I lied.

A total look of surprise puckered her lips. “I’m surprised

Josh has *any* friends."

Josie rolled her lip ring between her thumb and index finger as she studied the monitor then scribbled down an address.

"Why is that?" I asked.

The woman slightly lifted one shoulder in a partial shrug. "Josh is a little *different*."

"How so?"

Karen and the other women in the office shared a telling glance. "He's a little odd," one of the other women said.

Josie handed me the note with the address, coupled with a disapproving look. A non-too discrete eye roll completed the attitude. I handed the note back to her and asked, "Will you add your number in case I have any more questions?"

She confirmed with a sharp glance then wrote her name and number beside Josh's address.

Maybe I should ask them to define *odd* and *different*? The two were fairly generic descriptions. Either could describe a number of personality traits. "Is there something wrong with him?"

The looks that went around the room were telling. Finally, Karen said, "From what we understand, he comes from a...kind of...backwoods family. He's not like normal college kids."

"Sheltered?" Most of the people of this entire area were backwoods but it didn't make them any less normal.

"Yeah, I guess that's one way to look at it," Karen said. She turned away to answer a ringing phone. The other ladies went back to work, too.

I thanked them then excused myself, anxious to pay Josh a visit. Outside, I'd almost made it to my car when Josie called to me. "Miss Logan, wait up."

She rushed over then took a deep breath to regroup. "I didn't want you to get the wrong impression of Josh. He's really a sweet guy. They're just—stodgy."

A smile crept across my face at her definition. It wasn't the word I would have used but it worked. "Do you know much about his and Scott's relationship?"

She crinkled her nose in an unsure manner. "Not really. I mean, I don't know if they're, you know, more than friends. But Scott's super friendly to everyone so I can kinda see where someone might misinterpret it."

Who was misinterpreting the relationship? Scott? But he'd told Sara about Josh. Or had Josh misinterpreted Scott's friendliness for something more?

The pieces weren't connecting. And the more pieces to Scott's disappearance I found, the more scattered they were becoming.

CHAPTER 11

I stared at the sticky note with Josh's address written in a playful script. Foundry Loop, Mt. Rogers, Virginia. A good hour and half drive from Brighton College. There was no phone number listed other than Josie's so calling to see if he was home wasn't an option. As I set the address in my G.P.S, I prayed he was.

I called Doretha on the way. Heart-thumping, hand raising mountain music with a line of praise thrown in boomed in the background. Ivy was going to have her soul saved or eardrums busted if Doretha had anything to do with it. "How's she doing," I shouted into the phone.

"Grumpy, but otherwise okay. I'm going to lay her down for an early nap right after lunch."

A tiny wave of guilt rippled in the pit of my stomach. If Ivy had gone to bed at her normal time last night, she might be in a better mood. Of course if Scott weren't missing, *I'd* be in a better mood. "I'm on my way to Mount Rogers and may be out of touch a few hours. I should be back later this afternoon and can pick them up at the regular time."

We chatted another minute then ended the call. Doretha

had always been my advocate, my cheerleader. But today, I detected a bit of annoyance. There was something in her voice I wasn't used to.

Around noon, I crossed the state line into Virginia. Rolling mountains filled my view like a visual surround sound. Thirty minutes later, the impressive peak of Mt. Rogers rose into the sky amid towering pines. Wild ponies grazed in a field, unfazed by the passing vehicle. As part of the Blue Ridge Mountains and Appalachian Trail, the mountain claimed the title of highest peak in Virginia. At 5,728 feet elevation, it still fell short of North Carolina's Mount Mitchell.

Like other areas along the parkway, many roads—gravel, paved, and dirt—snaked their way deep into the forest, their ends hidden by the Fraser firs and rhododendron. The deeper into the woods the roads ran, the bigger the stories grew. Backwood hillbillies with rotting teeth, a long gun propped at their side, protecting the stills their granddaddies engineered. Nowadays, it was pot fields and meth labs they watched over. Some of the legends were true; most were not.

The G.P.S. indicated a crossroads a mile up ahead but a mile came and went. Two miles, then three miles around curves and switchbacks so deep you could easily become disoriented in the direction you were traveling. After another mile, I took a paved road that looked somewhat inhabited, hoping to find a glimpse of humanity. The road leveled out and emptied into a small village. A strip shopping center with four brick storefronts, including a grocery store, sat next door to a white-washed clapboard building with shuttered windows. A few older model cars and pickup trucks occupied the shared parking lot. Across the street, century old mill houses sprouted from the side of the mountain like mushrooms clustering around a mossy oak. The mill itself sat deserted like so many others in this region. When the jobs left, the people followed.

I pulled into the gravel lot and parked. There wasn't a soul to be seen, yet I felt eyes on me. Tourist overlooked these areas of the mountains, the ones tucked so deep into a way of life there was no escape. That was fine by the folks who lived in the hills and hollers. Always wary of outsiders, they trusted few but understood the language of the next mountain. The kinship of being misunderstood.

I walked the short length of the so-called shopping center, stopping at the barber shop. An old barber's pole mounted on the brick beside the door had seen better days, much like the village itself. The outdated inside transported me back to the 1960s. Maybe the 50s.

Two men as old as the mountain from which they came, sat along the painted plywood wall in a row of seats confiscated from a theater. Aged and weathered with buzz cuts, they wore short-sleeve button down shirts with breast pockets to stash a pack of cigarettes or pair of black-framed glasses. The one on the left wore such glasses although their eyes had lost their luster years ago. They sat stooped over, the harsh weight of simply living having taken its toll.

The barber was perched in the lone vinyl chair reading *The Roanoke Times*. Not quite as old as the other two men but still probably pushing seventy, he looked at me over the top of the paper. "Help you?" He asked, not bothering to put the paper aside.

"I'm looking for Foundry Loop."

He cut a glance at the other two men then folded the paper and tossed it on the counter. "Foundry Loop, huh?"

"Going to see Raeford, are you?" One of the men asked.

"I'm looking for Joshua Bloom."

The other one leaned in to the first one. "Raeford's boy," he said in what might have been intended to be a whisper.

"How do I find Raeford, or Joshua?"

The barber leaned forward and pointed out the dust-covered window. "That white building right there—that's his church. If there's an old station wagon or a pickup truck parked 'round back, reckon you found him."

"I'm not really looking for the father. I'm looking for Josh."

"Reckon you might find him at the house, then."

"On Foundry Loop?" I asked.

"On Foundry Loop. Go 'bout half a mile the way you came. There'll be a dirt path on your left with a cattle gate. You'll have to get out and open it if it's closed—"

"But close it back when you pull through," the one with the glasses said. "Raeford likes it closed." He and his friend shared a nod as if they'd shared a hidden truth.

The barber continued with his directions. "Go through the gate then the house is 'bout half a mile or so up the trail. If he ain't at the church, you'll find him there."

I wasn't going through the whole Raeford or Joshua thing again so thanked them and headed back to the Tahoe. Out of curiosity, I circled the white-washed building the barber had referred to as Raeford's church. The parking lot empty of a station wagon or any other cars, I assumed Reverend Bloom wasn't at his chapel. The shuttered windows prevented me from seeing in. Even the front of the building, an old store of some kind, was shuttered. No welcoming sign or hours of service anywhere to be found. No indication at all it was even a church.

But truthfully, that wasn't so unusual. Doretha's church had humbly began in Theo Parker's old Feed & Seed. When available land to build on was sparse, you used what you had. Besides, churches, like other businesses, suffered when the economy turned bad. When the congregation shrank, so did the bank account.

I made my way back to the Tahoe, still feeling their eyes on me watching every move. The barber said to go back the way I came—how'd he know which way I came? Because the locals know everything. And they tell no secrets.

But true to the barber's words, a dirt path up the road was closed off by a faded and chipped orange cattle gate. With no lock, opening and closing it back was easy enough. About fifty yards up the drive, three massive mixed-breed dogs rushed the Tahoe, snarling and nipping at the tires. Choke collars dangled loosely from their thick necks. Instinctively, my right hand moved to the glove box and fingered the Glock. I took it out and laid it beside me in the passenger seat, just in case.

The dogs continued their territorial display until we came to a clearing opening up into an unkempt front yard. A man wearing olive green work pants stood on the stoop of a brick ranch home with sun-faded shutters. He called the dogs off. They trotted over to him but continued to watch the Tahoe suspiciously.

An old station wagon with wood side panels was parked in the yard. Beside it sat a pickup truck, the tailgate down and bed exposed. Yard and garden tools lay in the back along with a couple discarded quarts of motor oil containers. Old truck like that probably burns the oil.

The man shielded his eyes from the glaring sun with a muscled forearm. "Can I help ya?"

Do I stick the gun in my bag? Just in case? He looked friendly enough, but the dogs still worried me. "They don't bite do they?"

"Not 'less you bite first." He offered a deep laugh then slowly approached the car. "I'm Raeford Bloom. And who might you be?"

I covered the gun with a jacket I kept in the seat for that very reason, then cut the engine off. "Ava Logan. Pleased to meet you Mr. Bloom, but I'm actually looking for your son, Joshua."

With the dogs uninterested, I got out and offered my hand. Although he shook it, his brows furrowed. "What'd ya need with Joshua?"

"Is he here?"

"I reckon he's around here somewhere."

We stared at one another for an awkward moment while he considered the stranger asking for his son, and I considered the cautious daddy. "Mind calling him for me?"

Raeford Bloom looked past me to the hills beyond, puckering his lips with skepticism. Not a bad looking man, he appeared to be early fifties with startling blue eyes. His auburn hair brushed the collar of his work shirt, shaggier than what I'd expect of a preacher. Sleeves rolled to his elbows displayed well-tanned, thick arms. I couldn't pinpoint the work uniform but figured preaching wasn't his full-time job.

He pulled his gaze away from the distant peaks and stared directly into my eyes with such intensity, a shiver traveled the length of my spine. "I'll be glad to call him for you, Miss Logan. As soon as you tell me why you need to see him."

The more Raeford resisted allowing me to see his son, the more determined I became. "He's not in trouble, Mr. Bloom. I just need to ask him a few questions about a mutual friend."

He blew a heavy breath then slowly nodded. "How rude of

me to not invite you in. Not very neighborly. Come on in and I'll let him know you're here."

Still on guard with the dogs, I kept close to Raeford as I followed him to the house. The black one with a white patch on its chest sniffed around my feet. Raeford shooed them away then held the door for me. "They look meaner than they are," he said and laughed.

I smiled politely, keeping the doubts to myself. Inside, Raeford motioned to an outdated and over-worn sofa. "Have a seat and I'll go get Joshua."

The living room was cramped and cluttered with too many side tables. They served no other purpose than to display various crosses, cheap decorative plaques with religious sayings, and ceramic praying hands. Two cane back chairs sat across from the sofa, positioned for conversation, not comfort. The house smelled old and dusty like a thrift shop.

I glared at a set of praying hands with guilt. Had I really interrupted my daughter's baptism? But we did find Scott's backpack, so it *wasn't* an overreaction on my part. Maybe if I kept telling myself that, one day I'd believe it.

Lost in my guilt, the sudden sound of someone clearing their throat startled me. I jerked my attention to a woman standing at the edge of the living room.

She nervously fiddled with a well-used dish towel. "I'm sorry, I didn't mean to scare you. I'm Susan."

After I introduced myself, Susan joined me on the sofa. Dressed in a denim skirt that fell mid-calf and simple plaid blouse, she looked dated and tired. Much like the house itself. No make-up, a wash-and-go hairstyle that could benefit from even boxed color, she was almost painfully *plain*.

"Raeford said you were here to see Joshua."

"Yes. I have a few questions I'd like to ask about a friend of his from college."

She wagged her hand toward the other part of the house. "Raeford went to get him. He's out back, mending the chicken coop."

Movement in the hallway caught my eye. A young boy and girl stood silently in the entryway staring wide-eyed at the stranger in their living room. The boy looked around Emma's age and possessed the same striking blue eyes as Raeford. The girl, much younger, sported blonde pigtails and a slender face dotted with freckles.

Susan turned to see what I was grinning at then smiled herself. "It's okay. You can join us," she said to them. "This is Joshua's brother and sister, Jonah and Rebecca. Can you two tell Miss Logan hello?"

Jonah didn't speak but those eyes screamed distrust. His sister squeaked a tiny greeting. Rather than coming into the living room, Jonah turned away and disappeared into one of the bedrooms. Rebecca looked like a baby deer alongside the road, unsure of which way to go. After a moment, she followed her brother's path and retreated to the same room.

Susan smiled politely. "We just finished today's lessons. I'm sure they're tired."

"Home school?"

"Yes. Raeford doesn't agree with the public-school curriculum." She smoothed her skirt although there was no need.

"Was Josh home schooled, too?"

"You mean Joshua. Yes. Yes, he was."

If he'd never been in a public school of any kind, Brighton College would have been a cultural shock. Although the college was private, it was still a college, ripe with near-adult kids tasting independence.

There was rustling in the kitchen then the sound of running water. Soon after, Raeford came into the living room followed by Josh. I recognized him from the picture Scott had shared with Sara. Taller than his father, he'd yet to grow into the fullness of adulthood. Hair the color of Rebecca's, but definitely his father's and brother's eyes.

I stood and shook his hand, although he appeared reluctant to accept the offer. "Hi Josh. I'm Ava Logan. A friend of yours worked—"

"Why don't we sit down," Raeford said, interrupting. He motioned for Josh to sit in one of the cane back chairs while he sat in the other.

Susan settled into the sofa, crossing her legs at the ankles. Obviously, this was going to be a family conversation. I sat back down beside of Susan but moved to the edge of the couch, closing some of the distance between myself and Josh.

"Scott Curry worked for me. I know that he was a friend of yours at college. He didn't show up for work last Thursday and I was hoping you might have an idea where he is."

He cut a glance to his father then shook his head. "The last time I saw him was about a week ago." Softness radiated from his voice.

"Did he say anything about going anywhere? Maybe to the beach with some of the other students?"

"He didn't say. But...I mean, he wouldn't have told me anyway."

Raeford laughed. "I'm sure he's with a group of buddies down at the coast. We'll need to get him in church when he gets back."

He let loose with a raucous laugh, even slapping his knee, as Susan responded with a shy smile. Josh flushed then attempted a grin. "Yeah, I'm sure he's with a group that headed for the beach. There was a big group going."

"You didn't go?"

"Joshua is needed at home during the summer," Raeford answered.

Despite having a chicken coop that needed mending, the property didn't look like a working farm.

For the first time since joining us, Josh smiled. "I also work some at the grocery store."

"Speaking of, he needs to get back to his chores." Raeford clapped his hand on his son's knee.

"Of course. I didn't mean to keep him." I dug a business card from my bag then handed it directly to Josh. "If you can think of anything that might help, please call me."

He studied the card a moment, sending a shot of fear through me that he'd hand it to his father. But he didn't. He slipped it into the back pocket of his jeans as he stood.

"Josh," I said, standing and stepping closer to shut out mom and dad. "Do you have a cell phone, or a landline? Some way that I can get in touch with you if I have any more questions."

Raeford stood, too, draping his arm around Josh's shoulder. "We don't have cell phones, Miss Logan. We do have a regular phone, though, if you'd like that number?"

Something told me speaking to Josh in private was going to be a challenge. If he and Scott were more than casual friends, his ultra-conservative family would be the last ones he'd want to know. "Yes, I would like the number if you don't mind. I'm sure I'll have other questions as soon as I'm on the road."

Raeford laughed. "Ain't that how it always works? Susan, get Miss Logan one of my cards, please."

Susan went into the kitchen then came back with a business card and a bible tract. "Our house number is that emergency number underneath the church phone. Preaching the word's a twenty-four-hour job." She handed them to me with the bible tract on top. "Do you go to church anywhere, Miss Logan?"

I wasn't sure how to answer. I fellowshipped with God on a hiking trail or on the river bank, not sitting on a pew in a man-made building. My relationship with the Almighty and his son was something deeply personal. Doretha and I often disagreed about it, but she respected my views, even if she didn't agree. "I have a home church," I said and hoped that would suffice.

"That's good," Raeford said. "Glad to hear it. Miss Logan you're welcome here anytime."

Despite being welcome, Reverend Bloom hurriedly ushered me to the door and walked with me to the Tahoe. The dogs followed, sniffing around my feet but remained calm.

"Joshua's a good boy." Raeford stood beside the car and spoke through the open window. "I was worried about him going off to college seeing how he's not *worldly*. He hasn't been experienced to the world like most college kids."

"They spoke very highly of him at Brighton." I left out the part about the ladies in the office saying he was different and a little odd. Something told me Raeford already knew that.

"He's paying for school with his own money. He works hard for it." Fatherly pride filled his honest words. Raeford rocked on the balls of his feet, staring at the ground like there was more he wanted to say but didn't know how.

"Is this his first year?"

"Second. He's a...what do you call that...a sophomore?" He

looked up and smiled at me and it was warm and genuine. "He's the first one in a long line of family to go to college."

"That's something to be proud of."

He slowly nodded. "My daddy and brothers and his daddy before him mined for coal over in Charleston. I won't gonna have none of that." He laughed but this time there was a sadness to it.

"Is that when you came here?"

He nodded again. "Worked in the mill 'til they closed it down. Shipped the jobs off overseas."

Unfortunately, I'd heard that song before. It was an all-too-familiar tune in these hills. "I'm sorry," I said truthfully.

"I better let you git. Hope you find that boy you're looking for."

"Thank you. I hope so, too."

He waited in the driveway until I'd turned the car around and had started down the long path before going back inside. I observed him in the rear view. Just standing there, hands in his pockets, watching me leave. I glanced over at the bible tract tossed in the passenger seat. *Repent now or burn in hell sayeth the Lord Almighty!*

If you can't save their souls with love, scare them to death. How sad people still believed in that theology.

Below the threat of eternal damnation, a cheap stamp read *Higher Heavens Holiness Church, Pastor Raeford Bloom.* Below that, two phone numbers and a bible verse indicator: Mark 16:17-18.

I made a mental note to look up the verse when I got home.

CHAPTER 12

Knowing I didn't have a cell signal coming down the mountain, I didn't bother to check my phone until I was well on my way home. Three voice mails—all from Doretha. My heart hammered in my chest as I hurried to punch in her number. There was no answer at the house, so I quickly hung up and called her cell.

After a torturous moment, she finally answered. "Been trying to call you. The call wouldn't go through."

"I'm sorry. I couldn't get a signal out. What's the matter?" I heard Ivy crying in the background. My pulse throbbed in my skull.

"Ivy has a double ear infection—"

"Did you take her to Doctor Morrow?"

"Urgent Care. Her fever shot up to a hundred-and-four and poor baby was in awful pain."

I squeezed my eyes closed, hoping to squeeze the guilt away. "I'm about forty-five minutes out. I'll be there as soon as I can."

"We're almost finished here so just come to the house. I need to get back before Emma gets out of school."

Emma. Another notch of guilt. Doretha had to take my

daughter to the emergency room, has to rush back to get my other daughter from school...because I was in the next state trying to coax words out of a kid whose father won't let him speak for himself.

"I'm sorry, Doretha. If I'd thought she was sick, I would—"

"It's okay. Just stop by the drug store and grab her antibiotic on your way."

After we hung up, I wanted to throw my phone. Damnit! I was batting two for three so how could I screw up something with Cole?

I settled into the guilt, accepting shit was going to happen and there wasn't much I could do about it. It came with the motherhood territory. Once my breath and heart rate returned to somewhat normal, I phoned the office.

Nola gave me the rundown of happenings, including a call from the sheriff. Why didn't Grayson just call me direct?

"Did he say what he wanted?"

"No. Want me to call him back and ask?" You could set your clock by the depth of Nola's southern accent. Up until lunchtime, she worked to keep it in check, careful with her pronunciations. After lunch, tire became tar and fire became far.

"I'll call him in little bit. I'm going to pick up Ivy and Emma and go on home. Ivy's got an ear infection."

"Oh poor baby. I hope she feels better soon. What are you going to do about the town council meeting tonight?"

My mind stopped. Screeched to a halt. "That's tonight?"

"Um...yeah. Did you forget?"

Yes. I did. "Oh, man. And they're hearing Bob Palmer's report on Mary McCarter tonight, too." I'll just have to ask Quinn to cover. I couldn't leave Ivy with Emma or Doretha, not with a fever and in pain.

I hated the days when the business owner in me and the single mother collided. There was never a good outcome.

When I got to Doretha's, Emma was in the old rocking chair with Ivy curled in her lap dozing. Poor baby's cheeks were deeply flushed and her forehead scorching. She started when I touched her then reached for me, puckered and ready to wail.

"I am sooo sorry, baby. I'm sorry you don't feel good." I lifted her and held her tight against my chest.

"The urgent care doctor said to follow up with her pediatrician," Doretha said. As soon as she handed me Ivy's bag, I remembered her medicine. And how I'd driven right by the drug store and still forgot to stop.

I didn't need a big scarlet A on my chest. I needed a big L for loser. I hurried Emma along and carried Ivy to the car, avoiding having to lie to Doretha when she asked me about the medicine. Although it'd be out of the way, I'd stop on the way home.

Doretha followed me outside, stopping on the front porch. "Call me later and let me know how she's doing."

I fumbled with the car seat, silently cursing the harness. "I will. Thanks again for taking her to the doctor."

In the car, Emma glared at me, unsmiling. "You forgot her medicine, didn't you?"

Most of the time, I enjoyed being a mother. Sometimes I didn't.

At home, I curled up on the couch in the sun room and lay Ivy down beside me. She still felt warm but not nearly as hot as earlier. She watched Bubble Guppies on Nickelodeon and attempted a giggle every now and then. Cole retreated to his bedroom and Emma did her homework at the coffee table while I read through the local zoning ordinances. I'd been running the paper and covering town politics enough years to almost know the ordinances by heart, but had to dig a little deeper to find the root of Nancy Farmer's concerns with Mary's homemade remedies.

Despite getting Quinn to cover for me at the council meeting, I still wanted to take lead on any article that may come from it. I wasn't sure Quinn fully understood the complexity of granny witches in these parts. I wasn't sure *I* understood. Mary's proclamation about a connection between my father and Scott still wormed its way into my conscience. *They're connected by evil.* Scott wasn't evil, but my father was. He'd been dead for years so how was there a connection?

From nowhere, the connection hit me. Scott wasn't evil. But something evil had happened to him. I prayed that wasn't the case as I grabbed my phone and called Grayson, easing myself off the couch, away from Ivy. Too wrapped up in the animated fish on the television, she paid me little attention.

As soon as he answered, I spilled what I suspected but hoped wasn't true. "If the connection is what Mary says it is, something bad's happened."

He hesitated before answering. "We have to look at all possibilities. But until we have a body, we're still looking at a missing person."

Emma's interest fell away from her homework as she turned a listening ear toward me. I moved into the kitchen and leaned against the counter. The bible tract from Higher Heavens Holiness Church glared at me from the side pocket of my bag. I took it out, remembering I was going to look up the bible verse, then went back to Grayson. "Are you still searching the river?"

"I called them off this afternoon. And we've got a BOLO on his car."

BOLO. Be on the lookout. It wasn't just for criminals. It sounded more final than I liked. "Then what do we do next?"

"*We* don't do anything. Steve Sullivan will conduct a missing person investigation."

A spark ignited in my stomach, burning a flame through the emphasis he put on the word *we*. "What does Steve Sullivan know about Scott Curry? Nothing, Grayson. He knows nothing."

"Ava—chill out. It's not like we're best friends with any of the victims."

Victim. The word felt nasty in my mouth. "But Sullivan? The guy's an ass."

"He's also a damn good detective. I'll tell him to keep you in the loop, okay?"

There was a big difference between Steve Sullivan keeping me in the loop and the sheriff doing the same. One trusted me. Sometimes.

It wouldn't do any good to pout about it. I'd just have to work around Sullivan. "Despite what either of you think, Scott's not a headline."

He sighed heavily enough for the sound to travel through the cell signal. "I know that. And whether you believe it or not, he knows it too. Look, I need to get inside. The council meeting's getting ready to start. Are you on your way?"

Finn turned circles around my legs, insisting on a treat. "Quinn's there. Ivy's sick so I stayed home with her."

Headlights shone through the kitchen window and for a second, my mind went to the gun safe. Cole bounded down the steps and burst into the kitchen full of smiles and AXE body wash. He kissed me on the cheek. "Thanks for keeping your promise."

I stared at the kid in the kitchen and wondered what he'd done with my son. "Hey, Grayson—I need to go. Call me after the meeting."

Before I could ask what promise I'd kept, Cole jerked the back door open and Finn started barking. A leggy blonde came up the back steps, all perky and bubbling with cuteness. Then I remembered what I'd promised.

Cole grabbed the girl's hand and all but dragged her inside. "Mom, this is Paisley. Paisley, this is my mom."

"It's nice to meet you, Miss Logan. I love the paper. My whole family reads it. My mom clips the recipes."

I smiled, awestruck this teenager was so polite, and she was my son's girlfriend. "It's nice to meet you, Paisley."

They went into the sun room, where Emma and Ivy were still, obviously in no dire need to be alone. I felt like a heel accepting gratitude for a promise I'd totally forgotten. If Ivy hadn't been sick, I'd be at the town council meeting and my son would be upstairs stewing over another broken promise.

So I wasn't exactly batting a thousand in the Mother of the Year award.

While I stood there, I looked up the bible verse on my phone. Mark 16:17-18. *And these signs will accompany whose who believe: In my name they will drive out demons; they will speak in new tongues; they will pick up snakes with their hands; and when they drink deadly poison, it will not hurt them at all; they will place their hands on sick people and they will get well.*

I stared at the tract, turning it over in my hand, searching for a hidden answer. Too tired to put much energy into it, I tossed it on the counter then rejoined the kids in the family room. I'd much rather watch colorful animated fish on television than think about demons and snakes.

CHAPTER 13

The next morning, Ivy's fever was down enough I wouldn't feel guilty for leaving her with Doretha. She crumbled her pop tart before devouring the sticky pieces. Cole watched her with amusement then shook his head and went back to his cereal.

"What'd you think of Paisley?" He asked around a mouthful of Cinnamon Toast Crunch.

I finished my coffee then rinsed the cup. "She seemed like a sweet girl." But I wasn't crazy about the fact she was a year older than Cole and came with her license and a vehicle.

At the moment I had other pressing matters. Like finding Scott.

Whether she was finished or not, I scrubbed the sticky from Ivy's face and chubby fingers much to her protest. I lifted her from her booster seat and dusted off the crumbs while Finn scarfed up the remnants. Emma helped me gather Ivy's bag on top of her own bookbag then held Ivy's hand while walking her to the car. "Medicine," she called from the back porch.

I grabbed Ivy's prescription from the refrigerator, hurried Cole along, patted Finn's head then finally made it to the Tahoe. As soon as I closed the door and buckled, Emma threw out a question that caught me off guard. "Why don't you get baptized with me when we reschedule, Mom?"

"Mom doesn't believe in baptism," Cole said.

I jerked my head around to stare at him. "Where'd you get that idea?"

"You told me the other day at the river. At Emma's almost baptism."

"You don't believe in baptism?" Emma shrieked.

"I didn't say that. I said I wasn't baptized in a river."

"So you have been baptized? You know you can do it more than once." Emma said.

I'd never been more anxious to drop kids at school than I was at that moment. My faith and beliefs were something I held close to my chest. I never understood the need to argue about whose God was bigger or to try and convince someone their religion was wrong. It wasn't that I didn't believe, because I did. I just opted to do it in a more private manner.

After depositing the kids where they were supposed to be, I swung by the office to check in before heading back to Scott's apartment. Danny Olson, my layout guy, was arguing with Quinn about a picture accompanying his article about dead snakes. Nola handed me a few message slips. I thumbed through them on the way to my desk.

Laurel View Insurance wants to change their ad. Again. Jackson Creek Elementary wanted to make sure we'd have a photographer at 5th grade graduation. Wilder Penzy has an idea for a story.

Wilder always had ideas for stories. No matter how many times I told him we didn't publish fiction, he persisted.

Quinn turned away from Danny and toward me. Hands spread, exasperated. Danny could do that to you, but he was a fantastic layout man. "Where does the image go if you're running it with a front-page article?" Quinn said.

I dropped my bag at my desk and joined them at Danny's work station. A mockup front page stretched from one corner of his hi-def monitor to the other. "So what's the question?"

"I have a great photo to go with the story about the dead snakes. Danny doesn't want to run it on the first page."

The snakes. I remembered the story well enough it brought on a nightmare. Jenkins Tooley came across a pile of dead snakes—rattlers, copperheads, even coral snakes—discarded like trash on Spearhead Mountain. It wasn't just the skins; the snakes were intact. The herpetologist Quinn interviewed said the snakes appeared older and malnourished. We chalked it up to a snake enthusiast who had no business with the reptiles.

Quinn had two pictures of the snakes. One was a shot of snakes where they were found, the second was the pile of snakes on a steel examining table with the herpetologist looking over them. "Danny wants to put the image with the continuation, not on the front page."

Danny's nose twitched. "Putting it on the front page makes the paper look like a grocery store tabloid. We might as well run a photo of Big Foot."

Quinn gasped, looking to me for justification, which I hesitated to give. They each had valid points, but my attention was so tunneled on Scott, I couldn't focus on a pile of dead snakes. "You know what—let's do this. Run the image with the story but bump the story to under the fold. That way it's not the first thing seen. Move the zoning board meeting above the fold."

Quinn waved his hand as he closed one eye. "Not so fast on

that. Mary McCarter's case was tabled until next month. The board wanted time to review it."

"So...not much of a story."

"Right. I could do just a general report, but I don't know that it's front page material."

I was glad for Mary that the case was tabled but aggravated that now we had to fill a hole. A curtain raiser wasn't front page news either, but it would give background on the upcoming case. "Why don't you do a background piece on Mary? About granny women in general."

His eyes widened. "You actually trust me with that?"

My stomach knotted as I struggled with control issues. I fought to convince myself it would be fine. Quinn was a damn good reporter. He was fair and experienced. I gnawed on the inside of my cheek before answering, finally giving in to the pain, and submitting to my little control problem.

I breathed deeply, relinquishing a little power. "There's another granny woman near the Tennessee line. Her name's Priya O'Conner. She doesn't have a phone, so you'll just have to ride over there. I'll text you her address."

Quinn didn't say anything for a moment, just stood there staring at me like I'd lost my mind. Maybe I had.

I went back to my desk and grabbed my bag, anxious to get out of there before I had a panic attack. Deep breaths. Deep breaths. Assigning this article to Quinn went against every deep-rooted control issue I had. He could do it justice. An outsider's perspective. It would be interesting to see it from a different set of eyes. I stopped at Nola's desk on my way out and handed the messages back to her. "Call Valley Ridge Insurance and tell Misty we need the ad revision before next Monday, call Susan Pritchard at Jackson Creek elementary and get the date and time of the graduation, and...tell Wilder Penzy, thanks but no thanks."

"Anything new on Scott?" she said.

"Grayson called off the river search."

"Well, on one hand we have to be glad he didn't find a reason to keep going."

And on the other hand—where is Scott? I left the office and drove to Scott's apartment, running the conversation with Quinn over again in my head. It actually felt good giving up some of the responsibility. It was just a tiny bit, but it was start.

At the apartment, I'd no sooner parked than the resident manager, Frankie Reynolds, opened her front door and peered outside. Still in her checked housecoat and bedroom scuffs, she disappeared back into her apartment. She came out a moment later waving the key. "I'm assuming you want back in his apartment."

We met up on the walkway. "I don't suppose he's been home?"

Frankie's arthritic hands must have been better today as she managed to work the lock herself. "Haven't seen him. How's the cat?"

"Hiding out in the laundry room."

She pushed open the door then followed me in. Nothing had been disturbed. Everything was still as it was. "What are you looking for today?"

Truth was, I didn't know. Maybe I just needed the connection? At the dinette table, I looked through the notepads and library books again. The books on snakes, wildflowers, and avoiding bears all made sense for a hiker. I stared at the snake book longer than the others, wondering, remembering the pile of dead snakes. Was there a connection? Probably not. I moved on to the other question and that one puzzled me even more. Why did Scott have a book on religion? He was studying pre-law and the last I knew, one didn't have much to do with the other. Was he trying to understand Josh's upbringing better? Learn about his background? I remembered the bible tract Raeford Bloom had given me. Higher Heavens Holiness Church. Holiness wasn't a mainstream denomination like the more prevalent Baptist or Methodist. But there were a lot of Holiness churches tucked into the hills, usually with small memberships that were family-centric. Was that what Scott was looking for in the book? I scanned the table of contents then read through the index. There was no mention of the Holiness denomination.

Frankie shuffled over to the table. "Rent's gonna be due soon. What do you think I should do?"

"I don't know, Frankie. Maybe his parents could help you with that."

I went into the bedroom, again looking for *anything,* ending up at his painted and scratched nightstand. A cell phone lay on top of a box of over-the-counter sleep aides in the drawer. What college kid would leave his cell phone in a nightstand drawer? Immediately, I took out my phone and called Scott's number. No ringing, no beeping. Nothing on the other line. I jerked up the phone and brought it back to life with the home button. With no password, getting into it was easy. The battery indicator showed red but still enough juice to last a few minutes. I found the charger at the bottom of the drawer.

Only one contact existed in the directory. Scott. I scrolled through the recent calls. All from Scott. It was too expensive to be a burner phone. Besides, why would he call his own phone over and over again? Unless it wasn't his phone. Then why was it here, in his nightstand?

I mentally backtracked the dates beside each call. The two most recent were from last Tuesday. Two days before Scott failed to show for work.

"Find something?" Frankie asked, peering over my shoulder.

I slipped the phone in my pocket. "I'm not sure."

Frankie tugged on the belt of her housecoat, her sagging jaw thrust forward. "Maybe you should give that to the sheriff's department."

I smiled, hoping to soothe her suspicions. "I know the sheriff personally. I'll make sure he gets it."

On the way to the McCarter's, Scott's extra phone taunted me from the Tahoe's cup holder. Maybe he bought the phone for Josh? It seemed possible, but still, it was in Scott's possession, not Joshua Bloom's.

When I made it to the end of the McCarter's dirt drive, Keeper came from around the back of the house. Unarmed this time. With a goofy grin spreading across his face, he waved his hand like he was directing a 747 on a runway.

He met me at the Tahoe. "Hey Ava! Momma—Ava's here." Neighbors two hollers over probably heard him.

Mary appeared at the corner of the house, the knees of her well-worn jeans caked in rich brown dirt. Her hair draped across a shoulder in a single braid. She wore work gloves and wasn't smiling. She spoke softly with no intention of the surrounding neighbors knowing she had company. "Keeper, go on and finish burying Charly. We'll say a word when you're through. He was a good ol' cat."

I jerked my attention around to Keeper as Mary

disappeared inside. “You found him?”

His usually happy face turned mournful. “Right where you and Sheriff Ridge was the other day, too. With the police dog.”

“Keeper, if someone killed Charly, y’all need to report it to the sheriff.”

“Momma says she don’t want no trouble. I gotta go bury Charly now.” He scurried off, more in a hurry to avoid the conversation than to do what his mother had instructed.

I hurried up the back steps. Even with nothing cooking on the stove, the temperature in the kitchen brought a sweat. A slight breeze filtered through the windows, barely moving the curtains. After pouring two glasses of tea from a Mason jar, Mary handed one to me then leaned against the counter.

The tea was sweet and cold, and very good. “You need to tell Sheriff Ridge about Charly.”

“I don’t want any more trouble than what I’ve already got.”

I understood her reluctance, but still, a crime had been committed against her. “Mary, whoever killed Charly should be punished. It was cruel. They probably did it to intimidate you.”

She gently swirled the tea in her glass, hypnotized by the tiny whirlpool. “They did it because they’re mean. Just let it go, Ava.”

“But—”

She held her hand up, long, narrow fingers bent with age. “I don’t really care what folks ‘round here think of me. But I’m going to be dead and gone one of these days. I don’t want my boy to suffer any more than he’s already going to for just being like he is. So, are you going to tell me the real reason for your visit?” Her voice floated in the air like a fleeting thought, just beyond total comprehension.

For a moment, I watched Keeper through the open window.

I didn't agree with Mary's reasoning, but I'd respect it. In a way, I admired the way Keeper's mind worked. Simple, uncomplicated. "The other day, you said Scott Curry and my father were connected by evil. I need to understand what you meant."

Mary sipped her tea slowly, her gaze fixed on a faded spot of linoleum. "It's just a feeling. They don't always come with an explanation."

"I don't understand how it relates to Scott. Scott's a kind, gentle, human being. Nothing like my father."

She shrugged. The frayed collar of an ancient Bob Dylan t-shirt slipped off her bony shoulder. "I don't know, Ava. Maybe you don't know him as well as you think you do."

Anger sparked from deep inside. "That's not true. There may be things I don't know about him, but I do know he's *nothing* like my father."

Mary sat the glass down on the counter then folded her hands. Quiet. Contemplative. "I won't argue with you. I'm just telling you what I felt. It's up to you to use it how you will. I'm going to go help Keeper. You're welcome to come along." She rinsed the glass then set it in the sink. The screen door groaned then fell as silent as the kitchen.

Born and raised in the hills, I understood the mystery of the gifts. I got it. But it didn't lessen the frustration. A deep sigh escaped my lips and I made no effort to suppress it.

Outside, Keeper shoveled a scoop of dirt into the small grave. A swatch of burlap poked up through the loosened brown earth. After another scoop, it disappeared, taking Charly's remains with it. When the grave lay level with the ground, Keeper tamped it down with his untied work boot.

Mary swatted at tears rolling over her hollowed cheeks. She

said a simple prayer in a voice barely there. “And although I’d rather hang the murdering sonsofbitches that did this, bless them Lord so that they might die with clean hearts.”

CHAPTER 14

My steps mimicked Keeper's as he returned the shovel to the tool shed. Close enough behind him, I smelled his sweat. "Who are the boys that told you they killed Charly? It's important, Keeper."

He shook his head hard enough, his ballcap fell askew on his head. "Momma says let it go."

I moved in front of him, forcing Keeper to look at me. "I understand. But this is about the young man the sheriff and I were looking for when we saw you in the woods. Maybe the boys know something about him, too."

"Momma don't want me to tell. She says—"

"I know what she says." I blew out a heavy breath while thinking of a way around his reluctance. "What if your momma says it's okay to tell me?"

Keeper's forehead creased with questions; his mouth morphed into a stern frown. "I don't know Ava. Momma don't want no trouble."

I placed my hand on his shoulder. Pleading? Maybe. At this point, I was desperate for answers. "I'll talk to your mother. You're not in trouble, Keeper. You haven't done anything wrong."

Poor thing. I felt responsible for the guilt shadowing his usually happy face. "Guess it won't hurt to ask her," he mumbled.

When we emerged from the tool shed, dark clouds had eclipsed the sky, bringing still air along with an ominous feeling. The first crack of thunder sent us scurrying to the house. Storms weren't in the forecast for the day but that obviously wasn't going to stop them from rolling in from the west.

Mary sat at the same table we'd gathered around the day of the showdown with Bob Palmer. She nibbled on a cracker while a butter knife protruded from a mason jar of homemade peanut butter. "Storm coming up?"

I sat beside her, helping myself to a cracker then slathering on the gooey brown spread. "Looks like it."

Keeper stood at the sink and made an attempt to wash the grave digging from his hands, distracted by the anticipated conversation between his mother and me. He'd cut his eyes to me, then to his mother.

"Keeper, would you like a cracker?" Mary asked, her gentle voice never wavering.

His excitement grew as he wiped his hands dry on his dirt-stained jeans. "Yes, please." He joined us, eager as a puppy for a treat. "Ava wants to ask you something, Momma. I tolt her you don't want no trouble."

Mary cast a glance my way while fixing her son his snack. "This about your missing delivery guy?"

"I'm thinking the boys who killed Charly may know something about Scott, too."

Skepticism? Or cynicism? One or the other spilled from her eyes and settled into a crooked smile. "What makes you think that?"

I chose my words carefully, not wanting to rat out Keeper any more than I needed to. "Scott's backpack was found in the river near the woods where Charly was found. Maybe the boys responsible for Charly know something about Scott."

Mary fixed another cracker without saying anything. She slid it to Keeper then fixed another for herself. A loud crack of thunder rattled the house. Soon after, rain pelted the tin roof. "Do you actually think someone cruel enough to torture and kill a helpless cat is going to tell you the truth about anything?"

Truth or not, I'd take anything at the moment. I could sift through the lies, bargain if I had to. I stood and pushed my chair under the table. "I can't just let it go, Mary. I'll find them with or without your help. I'm sorry about Charly."

I had turned to leave when she said softly, "The Blevins boy."

"It was him and his cousins," Keeper said, his voice brimming with a newfound eagerness. "Three of 'em. I counted."

"Troy Blevins?" I delayed my dramatic exit and sat back down.

"That's him." Keeper scooted his own chair closer to the table, excited now. "Troy Blevins. He has brown hair."

The kid and his cousins had been in one or another form of trouble their entire lives. Mostly petty stuff with nothing serious enough to send them to jail for even an overnight stay. Torturing and killing an animal seemed extreme even for them.

I turned to Keeper. "Troy told you they killed Charly?"

He nodded quickly. "Yep. Said they kilt him 'cause my momma was a witch."

Mary exhaled heavy enough the sound lingered. I still didn't understand the total connection. Most people in these parts knew of Mary's gifts and either believed or didn't. But those that didn't usually left her alone. Except the Nancy Farmers of the world.

"Which of Troy's cousins were with him?" I asked.

"Austin and Fletcher."

The branches to Troy Blevins' family tree began to spread out. But one limb demanded my attention. Fletcher Hanson was Carlyle Hanson's boy and Carlyle was the one behind Nancy Farmer's push for the zoning regulation. Those pieces began to fall into place. How Scott fit into the picture, or even if he did, was still a puzzle.

"What happened with Fletcher?" I asked, my question pointed at Mary.

Mary considered her answer before speaking. When she did, she spoke softly. The rain battering the metal roof nearly drown out her voice. "He didn't follow directions."

"What did he come to you for?"

"His momma brought him," she reflected. "Chronic nosebleeds. Said they'd been to a specialist in Boone and down to Asheville and no one seemed too concerned."

"What happened when he came to you?"

She pulled the knife from the mason jar and set it aside, then recapped the peanut butter. "I gave his momma Cardinal Flower and told her how to make the tea. I told her to be careful with it, that it could be toxic. Fletcher probably tried to get high off of it."

That didn't surprise me. There were those who looked for any high they could get. Opioids, heroin and fentanyl cocktails, meth. Gone were the days of smoking a joint for a giddy buzz.

"So, what happened?"

She lifted one shoulder in a methodical manner, like the

burden weighed her down or she no longer gave a damn. Probably a little of both. “Carlyle paid me a visit. Said I nearly killed his boy with my *brew*.”

Keeper sat up and pushed his chest out, rooster like. “He was all red-faced and huffing and puffing, too. Talking all loud at momma.”

Mary reached over and patted her son’s hand. “Don’t go getting riled up. It’s over.”

Keeper shook his head, lips pursing and pulsing with rising anger. “Ain’t over. They kilt Charly. And I’m gonna kill them back.”

Mary grabbed Keeper’s hand, her firmness making a point unto itself. “I say it’s over, Keeper. Let it be.”

He sunk low in the chair and folded his arms across his chest. His bottom lip protruded in a serious pout.

Mary turned her attention back to me. Annoyance glowed like embers in her eyes. “See why I didn’t want to bring it back up?”

Although killing the McCarter’s cat was despicable, my biggest concern centered around Scott’s disappearance. “If Keeper could just show me where he found Charly—”

Her hand shot up to cut me off mid-sentence. “I don’t think you understand what I’m saying, Ava. I don’t want my son involved. At all.”

“But Momma—”

The hand went up again as Mary shot a burning glare in my direction, the chastised child. “At all.”

Point taken. Loud and clear.

CHAPTER 15

Troy Blevins lived deep in the woods in a ramshackle house with his drug-addled mother and three younger siblings. My son Cole used to tell me Troy stories of when they went to school together until one day Troy stopped going. Two years older than Cole, the Blevins kid had been held back twice and rather than repeat again, tossed hope and a future out the broken window.

I sat in the Tahoe staring at the dilapidated home at the end of the dirt driveway. Would Troy retaliate against Keeper? That's the last thing I'd want. But I couldn't ignore that Troy and his cousins might have seen something in those woods.

Fingers grasped a tattered bedsheet in the front window, pulling back just enough to let the peeper see who had pulled into their drive. After a moment, the curtain fell back into place. I waited for someone to come to the door, eventually giving up on the Blevins' hospitality.

Three mixed breed dogs sauntered out from under the front porch with little interest in the stranger approaching the house. One sniffed at my legs while another squatted to take care of business. The third yawned then crawled back through the hole in the broken lattice work.

I sucked in a deep breath and climbed the rickety steps. There was no screen door. Just as I drew back to knock, the door creaked open. Jessica Blevins stared at me through eyes wishing for death.

We'd gone to school together. She'd been on the Homecoming court our sophomore year. I forced words up out of my throat. "I'm looking for Troy."

Jessica looked at me like there might have been a hint of recognition through the opioid-haze. The memory gone, she turned away from the door and moved slowly back into the darkness. "Troy Dean. Lady here to see you," she mumbled.

She'd left the door open, so I stepped through. The house smelled old and moldy, like a damp basement. Cigarette burn marks spotted the outdated shag carpet. Worn through to the backing, the dingy gold carpet had lost its nap around the same year I was born. I wondered if I should call out for Troy myself. I wondered if he'd heard his mother at all? Someone had heard her: a set of striking hazel eyes set in a cherub face peered around the corner. Dried jelly stuck to her chin. She scratched at a scabbed over bug bite on her skinny leg. It was hard to judge her age. So tiny. Maybe six? Seven? She should be in school.

A moment later, Troy Blevins appeared behind his younger sister. He moved her out of the way. "Go finish your lunch," he said, his voice firm but gentler than I would have expected.

He stepped into the living room, arms crossed. Attitude spilling from a go-to-hell expression. Shaggy bangs only partially covered the deep lines already creasing his forehead, making him look much older than his seventeen years. I searched the empty eyes for the little boy who used to play t-ball with my son, but he wasn't there. "You're the newspaper lady."

"Yes. Ava Logan."

Jessica came back to life and jerked her head from the armrest of the thread-bare sofa. "Ava Logan. You were Ava...." She struggled to bring the memory to the forefront of her faltering brain.

I helped her out. "Collins."

Her head moved in a slow bob as she put the face to the name. "Yeah. Ava Collins. You married...he played football...." She slurred through a mouthful of cotton.

"Tommy Logan."

Again with the slow head bob. "Yeah...that was him. Y'all still married?"

My heart hitched for a second. Who was more cocooned in their own little world? Jessica Blevins for not knowing Tommy had been gunned down in the line of duty? Or me for expecting her to know? "He's dead."

Her hollow eyes widened followed by a blink. "Oh. Too bad."

Troy reminded us he was in the room. "Yeah, so what do you want with me?"

I forced my attention on the angry-looking man-child and away from his mother. "Can I speak with you outside?"

He threw a harsh look at Jessica then moved past me to the front door. "Watch Cassie for a minute, will you?"

I followed him outside, glad to breathe in the fresh air. As I started to close the door, he stopped me. "Leave it open. I want to be able to hear Cassie."

He bounded down the few steps and grabbed a bacteria-laden water bowl from underneath the porch. A splash of green-tinged water hit the ground as he dumped what remained. The three mutts crawled out into the open and sniffed around the puddle. Troy shooed them away before rinsing the bowl at the lopsided spigot. They drank greedily when he plopped the bowl on the ground.

I looked back through the open door, at the skinny little girl who deserved so much more. “Why isn’t she in school?”

“Why ain’t you at work?”

I bit my tongue then took a deep breath.

“So what do you want?” He rubbed his hands on his too-big jeans, adding to the dirt and muck already caked in. They hung loosely on his sharp hips, plaid boxers with a frayed, stretched waistband visible like he was urban cool. Truth was, the jeans didn’t fit him. It was more a poverty statement than a fashion statement.

I joined him in the yard. “A few days ago, you were seen around Spearhead Mountain.”

He dug a crumpled pack of cigarettes from the front pocket of his jeans, pulled out an off-brand smoke and lit it. “What of it? Go there a lot.”

“You and your cousins?”

His eyes narrowed, heavy brow creased. He studied me as much as I was studying him. “We hang out.”

“Did you see anything out of the ordinary a few days ago?”

He crossed his arms and cocked his head back, attitude clogging his pores more than they already were. He blew a cloud of smoke in my direction. “What are you getting at, lady?”

“Someone went missing last week. We have reason to believe they were in that area.”

“So.” He took a long pull off the cancer stick. Like this kid didn’t have enough to battle, why not add lung disease to his future?

I steadied my breath, fighting the urge to smack the cigarette out of his hand. “Maybe you didn’t hear the part about someone missing. Someone that could be in danger."

He shrugged in a tough-guy kind of way. "Like I said, so."

I refused to look away from this kid. He wouldn't get that satisfaction. "Look, Troy. Someone is missing and you were seen in the general area—"

He flushed with anger, setting his jaw in defiance. Then he laughed and my skin sprouted goose-bumps. "That retard been telling stories again?"

My fists clenched so hard, my nails dug into the tender flesh of my palms. I counted to ten and sucked in a belly deep breath. My mind scrambled for an answer that wouldn't implicate Keeper. And I was coming up blank.

Troy spit on the ground near my feet. Flicked his cigarette into the dead grass. "Yeah, that's what I thought." He dragged each word out into exaggerated syllables.

"This isn't about that *retard*. This is about a missing person. You were seen in the area they may have gone missing in. If something bad's happened, the sheriff's going to be real interested in who was in the area. You and your cousins aren't exactly stellar citizens so who do you think the sheriff's going to want to talk to? Now, you want to cut the bullshit?"

He bellowed a laugh and my anger rose even more. "Look at you—getting all tough and all. Kinda cute when you're all pissy."

Before I knew it, I was in his face, inhaling the stench of his ashtray breath. "Look you little shit, I know what you did to the McCarter's cat. Are you too stupid to know that's a felony?

We stood toe-to-toe. My chest pounded in my ears with anger, and fear. My insides trembled thinking about this kid's reputation and here I was challenging him. I was too far in to back down. *Don't let him see your fear.*

After what seemed a lifetime, Troy took a step back, looked

away. He lit another cigarette, hands slightly shaking. "I didn't kill no cat."

My pulse settled as he took another step away. "But you were with them. That's accessory to a felony. You'll pull time for that, Troy." I was walking a tightrope of lies, hoping he wasn't savvy enough to know the truth.

He considered his imaginary fate as a flush rose in his cheeks. "I'm telling you—I didn't kill no cat."

"Who did? Fletcher? Austin? Doesn't really matter. All three of you will go down for it."

The flush faded quickly, replaced by a sickly paleness. "Look lady, we ain't got nothing to do with that missing guy."

"How 'bout we do this—I won't report how you and your cousins tortured and killed a helpless animal if you tell me what you saw?"

He guffawed, his mouth curled into a snarl. "Why don't you just go on back down the mountain. Tell the retard to mind his own business."

He stared hard straight into my eyes, probably wanting to do to me the same thing they did to Mary's cat. Even with the early summer heat bearing down on us, a chill tickled my spine. Troy finally broke eye contact and brushed by me. "I need to tend to Cassie."

I hurried after him up the steps. "Troy—wait."

He spun around, his face dangerously close to my own. His lips curled into a threatening sneer. "I don't know nothing about anything. Now go."

He took a step backwards and then slowly closed the door, maintaining the glare until the barrier separated us. My hands itched to knock again as the conversation wasn't over. Troy Blevins knew something about Scott's disappearance. How involved he might be remained to be seen.

I climbed back into the Tahoe more determined than deterred. There had been three boys involved with whatever happened in those woods: Troy, Fletcher, and Austin. . One down and two to go.

The afternoon was slipping away. I texted Cole, hoping he had his phone on even if he was still in class. Fingers crossed I could even get a signal out this deep in the mountain.

Is Fletcher Hanson still in school? I breathed a sigh of relief when I received a delivered status.

I stared at the screen as if that would make him reply sooner. Growing impatient, my finger hovered over the question mark when he responded.

What?

Is Fletcher Hanson still enrolled at school? Drop out?

Still here. Okay if Paisley comes over tonight?

The last thing I wanted to deal with tonight was another teenager. Usually quick to tell him no, I did hesitate this time. Paisley was a charming kid, and she genuinely seemed interested in helping him study.

Ok but she has to leave by 9:30.

THANKS!

I dropped my phone into the cup holder and watched as someone in the Blevins' house nudged the sheet covering the window aside. They let it fall back into place when I started the engine.

School let out in an hour and I needed every minute to get back to Jackson Creek. I turned the Tahoe around and headed down the mountain.

CHAPTER 16

Sitting in the parking lot at the high school, I scanned Snapchat for Fletcher Hanson. It'd been awhile since I'd seen him. Recognizing him without someone pointing him out might be a problem. I didn't find him on Snapchat so I tried Instagram and there he was.

A mass of auburn curls framed the round face of a boy not quite a man. He had Nancy Farmer's hooked nose. I locked up the Tahoe then went inside. The administration was used to seeing me at the school as a reporter so buzzed me in without question. The combustible energy of teenagers hovered like unseen fumes in the empty hallway. As the end of the school year drew near, the excitement jumped a notch each day. With fifteen minutes before the bell would ring, I went to the office.

Lexi Kantor, the student helper, smiled from behind the chest high counter. "Hey, Miss Logan. Are you here to meet someone?"

I stepped to the counter and spoke in a quiet voice. No need to involve an administrator who might have questions I had no answer for. "Could you call Fletcher Hanson for me?"

"Sure." She keyed his name into a computer then

summoned him through the P.A. system. "Fletcher Hanson to the office, please. Fletcher Hanson to the office."

I milled around the office while I waited, purposely avoiding the paid administration by feigning interest in a PTA flier. The fewer questions, the better. With five minutes before the bell, Fletcher strutted in. Shorter than social media made him appear, he threw me a glance then leaned into the counter and smiled at Lexi. He appeared to have a better life than his cousin Troy. Nicer clothes, well feed. Healthy except for the glassy eyes.

"What's up, Beautiful?"

Lexi didn't seem as impressed as he'd probably hoped. "Miss Logan from the newspaper is here to see you." She pointed in my direction then turned her attention to the computer.

Fletcher tried his charm on me. Broad smile through bloodshot eyes. "You gonna interview me for the paper?"

I smiled back then nodded toward the door. "Can we talk outside?"

He slung his book bag over his shoulder and then held the door for me. We moved along the walkway toward the parking lot. The shrill bell rang, vibrating through the concrete.

I steered us toward a bench under a pink crepe myrtle to avoid the foot traffic. "We're going to get run over. Mind if we sit for a minute?"

He tossed his book bag to the ground in front of the bench and sat down. "What's this about?"

I sat beside him. "An employee of mine has gone missing. They may have been around Spearhead Mountain before they disappeared. I know that you and your cousins were in the same area and am looking for any information you might have."

A slight breeze rustled his mop of curls. His brows knitted as his mouth curled into a tight frown. "What kind of information?"

"Anything. Did you see anything out of the ordinary? Hear anything?"

His eyes widened with surprise while the cockiness slipped away. "Not that I remember. We see people on that trail all the time."

"And you don't remember seeing anything out of the ordinary?"

Fletcher shifted his weight on the bench, shifted his focus to the ground. Blood trickled from his nose. He pinched his nostrils together then wiped the blood on his shorts. "Like I said, we see people up there all the time. Look, I wish I could tell you more, but I need to get home." He got up quickly and grabbed his book bag then gave me a thumbs up. "Hope you find him."

As he trotted off toward the student parking lot, the phone came out. I didn't need to see the contact name to know who he was calling.

I sat there on the bench for a few minutes watching the students scurry to their buses or their cars. Some were in a hurry. Others strolled along at their own pace, oblivious to the time constraints of others. Self-absorbed, existing for themselves, maybe a select group of friends. Whether Troy Blevins gave up being a teenager on his own accord or had to step up when his mother crashed and burned, I didn't know. I imagined it was hard to think about a prom date when you had to make sure your little sister ate that day. Was his anger justified? Maybe. It was still no excuse for the things he'd done.

I waited for the after-school traffic to die down then

returned to the Tahoe and headed back to the office. A feeling of defeat settled over me like a heavy blanket. The only thing I'd accomplished was to raise Troy Blevins' ire, tip off Fletcher, rat out Keeper, and royally piss off Mary for involving her son.

And Scott was still missing.

On the way to the office, my phone chirped several times notifying me of a new voicemail. A voicemail? To my knowledge, I hadn't received a call. I risked a glance and panicked when the message indicator showed three missed calls from Doretha. I quickly punched in her number without listening to the voicemail.

My heartbeat rose the same as the tone of my voice. "Hey, I just saw I missed a call. What's going on?"

Ivy cried in the background and my heart sank. "I'm at Urgent Care. Ivy's —"

Scared, I blurted out, "which one? Banner Avenue or Valle Cruces?"

"Valle Cruces. Ivy—"

"I'm on my way." I jerked the Tahoe into the left lane, ready to make an illegal U-turn.

Doretha huffed loudly followed by a shout. "Will you listen a minute? We're getting ready to leave."

My chest burned with the hurt of an embarrassed child. Yet, it was Ivy who was obviously hurt. "Is she okay?"

"Strep throat on top of the ear infection. Fever shot up right after lunch. I called her pediatrician and they weren't able to see her. I called you a couple times, but it kept going to voicemail."

I wanted to cuss the mountains I loved so much. The mountains I also hated. The mountains that stripped Troy Blevins of a future and blocked cell signals that needed to get through.

Doretha continued. "She got another prescription, so I'll drop it off, and then I'm going to take her back to the house. Can you pick up her medicine on your way?"

"Yes, of course. I'm on my way now. I'll get it when I pick her up."

She was coaxing Ivy into her car seat with a grand-motherly voice. Then, she said, "I called Jeremiah to the house to sit with the others. Emma should be there by now, too."

Jeremiah. The church elder who gave me the stink eye every time he saw me. I couldn't wait for the condescending glare that I knew would come with this latest issue. "Thanks, Doretha. I'm sorry you had to—"

She cut me off. "No worries, Baby Doll. Ol' Doretha's got it handled. See you in a few minutes."

Doretha clicked off her phone and I sat in traffic staring at mine. What if it'd been more than an ear infection and strep throat? Cole and Emma had reached the age, the tether had thinned. I was seldom out of touch by more than an hour, but I no longer worried about them as I did when they were babies. Like Ivy.

The driver of a Dodge truck behind me laid on the horn. I hurried through the light then turned onto Main Street at the next intersection. A small cluster of teenagers gathered on the sidewalk at the V & V Market. Hanging out at the Value and Variety was the thing to do now after school. The owner, Waylon Breker, was none too happy about it, calling them *hoodlums*. He'd asked me to do an article on it, the loitering, hoping the kids' parents would see it and insist their children come straight home.

I'd asked if the kids were stealing from him, shoplifting maybe? Or vandalizing the property with graffiti? Turns out

Waylon's daughter and one of the boys were an item. Waylon was more upset about that than the loitering.

I wondered how Paisley's parents saw Cole? Did they look at him the way Waylon looked at the boy chasing his daughter, like a circling wolf? Full of threat and trouble?

Last year, with the investigation into the death of Ivy's birth mother, I discovered things about Cole I hadn't known. Anger turned to rage then settled into reluctant acceptance when Grayson assured me my kid was normal.

After arriving at Doretha's, I hurried inside and went to the kitchen. In the attached dining room, Doretha barked homework orders at the older ones while the little ones begged for snacks. Jeremiah dished out Goldfish and juice in between giving me the evil eye. He sang "Down by the River to Pray," probably on purpose as a reminder of my other failure. I scooped Ivy up into my arms, pressing her cheek to mine. She was burning up. "Oh baby, I'm so sorry you don't feel well," I whispered.

Emma hovered like a miniature mother, gently stroking Ivy's blonde curls. "I tried to give her some juice, but she didn't want it."

Doretha pointed one of the kids to a chair at the table. "Poor thing's throat's hurting."

I pulled away from Ivy's cheek and looked at her cherub face. Flushed and red-eyed. "Does your throat hurt?" We were still working on the basic body parts—why did I expect her to know where her throat was? It'd been several years since I'd had to translate toddler speak.

She burrowed into my shoulder and squeezed my neck with her chubby arms.

"Poor baby," Doretha said. "She was plum pitiful at the

doctor's office."

I should have been with her. What if it had been a life or death situation rather than a common ear infection and strep throat? I shoved the thoughts aside having played the guilt game one too many times before. "Thank you for taking her."

Doretha nodded, meeting my eyes with her own then giving me a wink. She understood. "I've had a few sick little ones in my days. Ol' Doretha knows what to do."

Emma finished packing Ivy's bag and slung it over one shoulder while her own book bag hung from the other. "What about tomorrow?" she asked.

"What *about* tomorrow?"

"If Ivy's still sick? Are you going to stay home with her?"

The question jabbed me hard in the chest. How many times had I dropped my kids off at Doretha's with fever, snotty noses or upset stomachs? Doretha had spoiled me as much as she had my kids.

Doretha jumped in and saved me, again. "We'll decide that tomorrow."

I thanked her with a tender smile and nod then herded my inquisitive twelve-year-old out to the car. Ivy balked and dug her baby fingers into my neck when I tried to put her in the car seat.

It was going to be a long night.

CHAPTER 17

On the way home, I picked up Ivy's new medicine and a pizza. While Emma and Cole devoured the pizza, I managed to get some applesauce into Ivy. She was beyond fussy. Even Emma, who too often jumped in to take up my slack, feigned homework and hid upstairs. For the best, I supposed. We didn't need strep throat making its way around the house.

I walked the floor of the sunroom with the toddler in my arms, head on my shoulder, and crying. Grant it the mind-numbing wails had settled into a heartbreaking whimper, but still, she cried.

Cole came in and paced with me. "Can you take her upstairs, or maybe in the living room?"

I understood what he said, but I wasn't understanding why. Emma had sought refuge in her bedroom. Why couldn't he do the same? "What's wrong with your bedroom?"

His eyes widened with surprise then the slightest of smiles made his lips twitch. "Sure. We can do that."

We? Paisley. I stopped pacing and stared at my over-eager son. "I forgot about Paisley. The bedroom's out."

Ivy lifted her head and whined, glaring at Cole through

glassy-eyes. She tugged on her infected ear. I resumed the baby-march, wearing a path in the carpet.

"Where are we supposed to study?" He asked, miffed at my non-working memory.

"The kitchen."

He huffed as only a fifteen-year-old can. "Mom—why can't we just study in my bedroom? All we're goin' do is *study*." Eye roll.

I stopped pacing and glared at my son. "I'm putting myself in her parents' place, Cole."

Again with the rolling eyes. He turned, stomping off, and mumbled, "Yeah. Whatever."

Any other day I'd have answered the attitude with a stern lecture about respect, maybe take away his phone. Today wasn't that day. One baby at a time was my limit and right now, Ivy demanded my attention.

I walked and patted her butt, my arms aching and legs tired. Emma had been prone to ear infections, and Cole strep throat. That was about the gist of their drama. I couldn't help but think of Scott's mother. The helplessness that glazed her eyes. And then there was Troy's mother, eyes glazed for a different reason. My heart wasn't bleeding enough for Troy, though, to ignore his involvement with the McCarter's cat or possibly Scott's disappearance.

Heat from Ivy's cheek radiated through my shirt and warmed my shoulder. She had settled into a light doze, minus the whimpering. Still, I walked and patted.

Finn lifted her head from her spot near the wall of windows, ears on alert. She followed with a *woof* then leapt up and darted for the kitchen. Seconds later, a soft knock on the door was followed by Grayson's voice.

"In here," I said quietly, hoping not to wake Ivy.

Grayson followed Finn into the sunroom, stooping to give the dog a vigorous pat. Satisfied with the attention, Finn trotted back over to her spot in front of the window and settled back down beside Boone. Grayson kissed me on the cheek and semi-wrapped me in a half hug. If my arms hadn't been full with a sleeping baby, I'd have returned the hug and gone in for a deeper kiss.

He gently touched her cheek with the back of his hand, his brows creasing. "She's hot."

"Ear infection *and* strep."

He nodded like he really understood, and it made me smile. No kids. Not even a dog. I carefully eased onto the sofa with Ivy still in my arms. She squirmed a little bit, her breath hitching in a tiny snore. Grayson sat beside me.

He asked, "Not feeling any better?"

"No. Her fever shot up again so Doretha took her to Urgent Care. They did a strep test and of course it was positive."

"Doretha took her?"

The sting of his unintentional judgement burned. I stroked Ivy's silky hair, a makeshift apology for not being there when she needed me. "I was on the road and couldn't be reached."

A tentative grin played at his lips. He sat beside me and draped his arm across the back of the sofa. "Chasing a story?"

Instantly, my stomach knotted. Troy Blevins and his cousins could provide information about Scott's disappearance, but animal cruelty was also a felony in North Carolina. If I told Grayson about Keeper's cat, the trio could face charges. And they would retaliate against Mary and Keeper. No doubt about that. "Just running down some leads," I said, comfortable in the truth. "What's the latest on Scott?"

The grin faded as he shook his head. "Sullivan's talking to people at the college. There's still been no activity on his debit card or cell phone."

"Cell phone! I almost forgot." I told him about the extra phone I found at Scott's and my suspicions. "If he bought it for Josh, then it makes sense that he'd be calling it, right?"

Grayson stared at me, brows raised. He pulled his arm away so he could turn and face me head-on. "Who the hell is Josh?"

I froze. My thoughts simply ceased.

"Ava?"

"Oh my God...Grayson...it totally slipped my mind." I spilled everything I knew about Joshua Bloom and how it related to Scott Curry.

"You didn't think it was something you should have told me before now?" His voice rose with something I wasn't used to hearing from him—anger.

I leaned away, staring hard at those Sinatra blues. "Wait a minute, Grayson. It's not *my* job to investigate this case for the Sheriff's department. You have Steve Sullivan for that."

"What about sharing of information?"

I stood, needing to put space between us. The conversation was creeping toward an argument. "That works both ways. You locked me out of an interview with Scott's parents."

He gnawed on his bottom lip. After a long moment of dead silence, he exhaled. Pushed his hand through his hair. "I don't want to argue."

Good, neither did I. But I wasn't going to kiss his ass, either. "I didn't withhold information, Grayson. I honestly forgot. I've had other things to deal with." I waved my hand in Ivy's direction, thankful she was still sleeping.

The stuff I'd gathered about Josh, about the cell phone,

about Scott's relationships—made me wonder just what Steve Sullivan was doing to find Scott. I understood police work enough to know looking into relationships would be a priority. His parents didn't know he was involved with someone, but his sister did. Had Steve even questioned Sara?

Grayson scrubbed his face with his hands, the tiredness tugging his mouth into a frown. "Do you have the cell phone with you?"

"It's in my bag." I retrieved the cell from my bag in the kitchen and handed it to him when I returned. "It's too expensive to be a burner phone."

Grayson stared at it, turning it over in his hand. He pressed the home button and the phone came on but gave a low battery warning.

I sat back down beside him. "The only calls on it were from Scott's cell phone."

His brows knitted as he scrolled to the recent calls list. "That matches Scott's cell phone record. There were several consecutive calls to a Boone area code. It must be the phone."

Grayson swiped screens until he found the info folder then opened it. The *My Number* tab showed the Boone area code along with the number.

"Same number?" I said.

He nodded but didn't say anything.

"Can the carrier tell you who the number belongs to?"

"Possibly. But, if Scott bought the phone to give to someone, it's going to be in his name, not the other person's."

"But just because Scott had it, doesn't mean he bought it, right?"

He laid the phone on the coffee table and stared at it like he was channeling the answers. "Obviously, getting a clean set of fingerprints off it is going to be issue."

Should I point out he'd handled it too? I swallowed the comment, needing to snuggle into him more than argue with him tonight.

"I've got some volunteers coming tomorrow to search the woods up river."

The same woods where we had run into Keeper. The same woods where Troy and his cousins had been up to no good. "What time are you doing that"

"We're going to organize at the fire department at nine."

I stroked Ivy's hair wondering how I was going to manage this. Unfortunately, Scott's upgrade to missing person status *was* newsworthy. If he turned up alive and well before the next issue of the paper went to press, which I truly hoped he would do, there wasn't a story. On the other hand, if he was still missing by press day, it was front page above the fold material. Like it or not, the publisher side of me couldn't ignore it. Nor could the mother side of me ignore the sick kid lying beside me.

I cuddled into Ridge, burrowing into his comfort. Every part of me longed for a night alone with him, even after our spat. The sound of Cole's tennis shoes slapping hurriedly against the hardwood stairs meant Paisley must have just arrived. Sure enough, a moment later Finn alerted with a yelping *woof*. I held my breath as Ivy startled. Thankfully, she settled and didn't wake. Finn got up without barking again and trotted into the kitchen as the back door opened and closed. Grayson pulled his arm from around my shoulder like we were teenagers about to get caught at something. "Expecting company?"

I couldn't stop the chuckle from escaping. "You're the only

company I ever get. It's probably Cole's girlfriend, Paisley. You can put your arm back now."

Before Grayson had the chance, Finn led Cole and Paisley to the entranceway where they stood, hand-in-hand. Actually, Paisley's hand, arm, upper body and right breast were hugging my son's arm. I smiled politely despite the urge to clear my throat and tell them to cool it with the public display of affection.

A toothy smile shown through Paisley's perfectly pouty lips. "Hey Ms. Logan. Sheriff Ridge."

A sweet kid, even if I didn't want to believe it. "Hey, Paisley."

"I saw you at school today talking to Fletcher Hanson. I guess you were on some big story, huh?"

My polite smile abruptly fell into a blank stare as my mind scrambled for a good excuse. Crap. Did I tell Grayson about Fletcher's involvement with Troy and the dead cat? "Yeah, I guess you could say that."

Cole had grown bored and tugged at Paisley's hand. "We'll be in the kitchen studying."

As soon as they disappeared, Grayson asked, "Isn't Fletcher related to Nancy Farmer?"

I took a breath before answering. "Yes. He's Carlyle's boy."

He took a deeper breath than I had. "And Carlyle is behind the zoning issues with Mary McCarter?"

"It appears that way." I explained the connection and how Fletcher's mother had sought out Mary's help. "Apparently, Fletcher thought the tonic was something he could get high off of and nearly overdosed."

Grayson stared with unflinching eyes. "Like the opioid epidemic isn't enough to deal with."

In that moment, I wanted to rattle on about Troy Blevins and his addict mother and how Troy was having to care for his younger siblings. I wanted to tell Grayson so he'd be obligated to contact DSS and help those poor kids. But telling him that would mean I'd have to tell him about the dead cat.

The secrets we kept from one another were becoming an issue.

CHAPTER 18

I woke the next morning with a chubby finger poking me in the eye. Sharing my bed with a toddler who has no sense of personal space resulted in little sleep. Still, I was happy to see her smiling.

"'Ime up," she said with another poke.

I felt her forehead with the back of my hand. Nice and cool. "My time's up?"

She cackled and fell back on the bed, clearly recovered. I couldn't contain the sigh of relief. First, for the fact she felt better, and secondly, I was spared the judgement I'd have inflicted on myself for leaving her again with Doretha when she was sick.

By 9 o'clock, the kids were dropped off at school, Ivy at Doretha's, and I was with Grayson and a group of volunteers at the Jackson Creek Volunteer Fire Department. Jeff Maness was there with his dog, Ruger. A Bloodhound from Wilkes County lay beside the shepherd while his trainer chatted with Maness. Keeper stopped sweeping the bay floor every minute or so to listen to Grayson. He'd cut a glance in my direction, then look away.

Reluctantly, I took a picture with my phone of the number of volunteers. As much as I didn't want to think like a publisher right then, it'd make a great visual for the story.

One of the volunteers, Patch Dolan, walked over to me. He was one of those whose age would be impossible to guess if he hadn't lived here all his life. You simply gaged the range from who he went to school with. Mid-forties, on his third marriage, and worked his jaw constantly like he was cracking a knuckle. "So what do you think happened to him?" He pushed his lower jaw to the right, then the left.

"I hope nothing."

"I think we all hope that." Again with the jaw. "I heard you drug his backpack out of the river. Interrupted a baptism or something."

I blew a shallow breath, hoping my legacy would involve more than interrupting a baptism. "Yeah. Or something."

The crowd broke up and hurried to their individual cars and trucks. Patch clapped me on the shoulder. "It's showtime. You gonna join the search?"

As a publisher, an employer, or just another volunteer? I wish I knew. "Yeah, I'm going." I'd figure out my role when I got there.

When Patch jogged over to his truck, Keeper rushed me. "Can I ride with you, Ava? Please? I won't be no trouble. Promise."

My lips wanted to smile but I didn't. "You're no trouble, Keeper. Just make sure it's okay for you to leave."

"Oh, I done finished my sweeping. Chief Grady said I could go after that."

I pointed at the side of the building, at the bicycle leaning against the brick. "Grab your bike and we'll throw it up in the back of the Tahoe."

A few minutes later, the caravan headed out of town toward Spearhead Mountain. Keeper fidgeted in the passenger seat, starting to say something several times only to remain quiet. He kept his right hand between the seat and the door, clearing failing at sneaking something on board.

After numerous false starts, I pursued. "What is it, Keeper?"

He sank back into the seat. "Momma says something bad's happened."

They're connected by evil. I pulled my attention away from the road for a second and stared at him. "Bad how?"

Keeper shook his head. "Must be bad bad. Momma tolt me to bring these with me." He pulled two metal rods out from their hiding place at the passenger door.

"Are those the—"

"Yep. Momma tolt me to bring them, too. Said it was gonna be bad."

I jerked my eyes back to the road, although my attention was on the grave dowsing rods in Keeper's hands. I hoped just once Mary was wrong.

The volunteers spread out in an organized radius from the first overlook at Spearhead Mountain. Grayson gave me a quick kiss before heading into the woods. I stood there watching him follow Maness, watching the others, disappear into the thick pine forest. At that moment, I wasn't anything. I wasn't a publisher, an employer, or even a volunteer searcher. What I *was* was scared.

Keeper rocked back and forth on his feet beside me,

anxious to put his dowsing rods to use. To put Mary's theory to the test. "We gonna go with 'em?"

I swallowed the knot in my throat. "I guess it'd be better than going by ourselves."

We headed into the woods, moving quickly to catch up. Any other time, I'd drink in the smell of the moss, embrace the closeness of the trees. Now, the all-encompassing cluster smothered me. I fought back the need to push my head above the tree tops and breath in the openness. Like fighting your way from underneath an old, heavy quilt, my muscles ached with frustration.

Feet snapping twigs, boots stomping over roots, the low drone of chatter, an occasional call for *Scott Curry*—it all amplified into a cacophony in my head. Even the birds' gentle sing-song melodies prickled my nerves. Close enough to the river, if I listened hard enough, I could hear the subtle roar of moving water.

Ruger circled back, his high wail echoing through the crests and valleys. The Bloodhound joined in from a distance then grew closer as he moved toward us in hot pursuit. Like a giant circle collapsing into itself, the group of volunteers looked from one to the other, their faces a canvas of concern.

"He's not there," Keeper whispered from behind me.

The dogs were hyper-focused on a spot in the middle of the circle of volunteers. Ruger barked an alert then lay down at Maness's feet, whining and pawing at the ground.

I turned around and stared at Keeper as he trailed a few feet away. He held a dowsing rod in each hand, arms extended as if he were carrying a tray. The movement was so slight if I hadn't been watching, I'd have missed it. The end of the rods came together, first forming a V, then overlapping until they formed an X.

Keeper looked over his shoulder at me, his face so innocent, almost happy he'd helped. "He's right here."

CHAPTER 19

Yellow tape stretched between trees, boxing off an area the size of a small house. Grayson conferred with Bosher Garrett, the Jackson County Medical Examiner, while a tech snapped pictures of the scene. The volunteers had been sent home with a vow of silence until an official announcement would be made. Grayson would contact the Currys first then issue a press release, which I would toss. At this early stage, what we didn't know was still much more than what we did. I didn't need a generic press statement to pen an article by. Especially this article. Despite my personal feelings about it, Scott Curry had become a headline. Front page, above the fold.

Keeper and I sat on a boulder and watched the scene unfold in front of us. An arm unearthed from a thin layer of brush and fallen leaves, the outline of the full body buried beneath plainly visible. The fact his body was covered showed either someone hoped to conceal the body, or they were remorseful for what they'd done. Or both. Either way, someone made an attempt to bury Scott's body. From where I sat, I couldn't tell if the marks on his arm were defensive wounds or maybe scratches from a bobcat or bear. The body was intact so the chance he was the victim of an animal attack was slim.

I thought of the Currys and the call they would receive. The tidal wave of emotions that would come with Grayson's words. Relief that it was over? It wasn't the answer anyone had wanted. Yet, it was an answer.

Grayson would extend his condolences to the Currys, but who would tell Josh Bloom? If his and Scott's relationship was as personal as Sarah Curry believed it to be, Josh deserved a similar courtesy.

I nudged Keeper then stood with urgency. "Come on. Let's get you back to the fire department."

His unkempt brows creased. "Sheriff Ridge might need us."

I gently tugged on his elbow. "Sheriff Ridge has it under control."

Keeper dragged himself up to his full height and frowned. "I might can get a ride with Sheriff Ridge."

I shook my head and nudged him forward. "That's probably not a good idea. He's going to be here awhile."

Once I got Keeper moving in the right direction, I motioned to Grayson to call me later. He nodded then turned his attention back to the medical examiner. I herded Keeper around the crime scene tape and back to the trail leading out of the woods, my steps wide and hurried. I wanted to get to Josh before the rumor mill got cranked up.

"I don't know why we can't stay," Keeper pouted.

I unlocked the Tahoe and slid in. Keeper climbed into the passenger seat. Still pouting. "We'd just be in the way, Keeper."

After dropping him and his bike at the fire station, I checked on Ivy before I headed too deep into no-signal territory.

Doretha said a prayer for Scott and the Currys when I told her the latest development. "You go on. You got a job to do. Ivy's fine. Besides, I can handle Miss Ivy."

A little while later, I crossed the state line, driving deep into the mountains of southwest Virginia and Mt. Rogers.

I slowed as the small shopping center came into view. Two elderly men sat on the bench outside the barber shop, shoulders stooped, almost parallel with the ground. They lifted their faded eyes to glare at the stranger driving past them.

My own gaze moved to the grocery store on the corner and the young man sweeping the sidewalk. Josh stared at me through the windshield, bringing the motion of the broom to a dead stop. He hurried inside and disappeared behind the double glass doors. I swung the Tahoe into the parking lot, hurried around the building then quickly pushed through the double doors behind him.

The store smelled like bleach masking the old and decaying. Florescent lights buzzed and flickered overhead, casting brightness in some areas, shadows in others. Old-school tile showed the wear of years of shopping buggies with bad wheels.

Two registers sat between the doors and the bulk of the store. A cashier who couldn't have been any older than Emma looked at me but didn't bother to smile any kind of greeting. Her dull eyes were lackluster orbs of boredom, or maybe acceptance that this was all there was.

"I'm looking for Josh."

She pointed a little-girl finger with a chewed fingernail then dropped her dead eyes back to the National Enquirer she'd been looking at.

I found him in the canned food section pretending to stick orange price tags on cans of green beans. He kept his gaze downward, the only acknowledgment of my presence was his rapid breath and trembling hands.

“Did y’all find Scott?” His voice was soft and low, not the booming fire and brimstone of his father.

I closed the distance between us. “Yes. He was found this morning. Josh—”

“Is he dead?” He stopped tagging the cans but continued to stare at the dusty tops.

I wanted to reach out and touch his arm, but I didn’t. “I’m afraid so.”

He nodded quickly and sucked in a deep breath. He then went back to putting the orange stickers on the green beans.

“I’m sorry, Josh. I know y’all were friends.”

After adjusting the pricing gun, he moved down to the canned corn.

“Scott’s sister, Sarah, told me y’all were close. She said Josh spoke of you often to her.”

He did a quick sweep with his eyes in my direction but didn’t make eye contact. Neither of us said anything for a moment. Finally, he wiped at his cheek with the back of his hand and spoke. “Why’d you come here?”

“I didn’t want you to read about it in the news or hear about it at school. I thought you deserved to know.”

He dropped the price gun on a rolling cart then hurried through the narrow aisle to the back of the store. Pushing through the swinging stainless steel doors, he swiftly moved around the stock and butcher’s area then shoved the back door open.

Outside, Josh bent over, hands on his knees, gasping for air. I wanted to reach out and touch him, to comfort him. To tell him I was sorry for his loss and I understood, and I didn’t judge. Instead, I shoved my hands in my back pockets.

After a few minutes, he straightened and sucked in a deep

breath. Tears dampened his crystal-colored eyes, making the blue glisten. He sniffled then asked, "How'd it happen?"

"We don't know yet. We'll know more after the autopsy."

He gave that some thought. "Do you know when it happened?"

I shook my head. "The medical examiner will be able to give us a better idea."

Josh leaned against the brick, taking a few minutes to collect himself.

When I felt the time was right, I asked, "Do you know if he was having trouble with anyone? A disagreement, heated words?"

He whipped his head around and glared at me. "Why would you ask that? You think he was *murdered*?"

I scrambled to cover myself. "We don't know for sure what happened. I'm just looking at all possibilities."

Did Josh think Scott may have taken his own life? The body was buried under leaves, purposely concealed. Unless Scott had taken his own life and someone, someone like Troy Blevins, had stumbled upon the aftermath.

"Do *you* think Josh may have taken his own life?" I said.

Josh looked away, his gaze drifting over the tree tops to the peaks beyond, lost in the blue haze of mountains. "Not really."

"Had he been depressed?"

"No more than...anyone else I suppose."

But not everyone takes that final step. They shake it off and go on. "When's the last time you saw him?"

He shrugged. "About a week ago."

"How'd he act?"

He mulled over his answer, chewing on his bottom lip. "He was upset. I told him we couldn't be friends anymore."

I tried to fit fragments of their relationship into a whole picture. Friends? Lovers? Or neither. Had Scott misinterpreted something that wasn't there? Judging by the pain evident in Josh's face, I doubted it. The boy was hurting, there was no question about that.

Despite his discomfort, I pressed. I wanted to know how Scott died, but I needed to know why. "Why couldn't you be friends with him anymore?"

Something weighed on Josh, beyond my grasp. Just as he started to speak, a station wagon turned into the parking lot and pulled to a stop beside Josh's old truck. Raeford Bloom, bible in hand, climbed out and headed our way. All smiles.

"Good day to you, Miss Logan," he said as he approached. "What brings you back to Virginia?"

I smiled politely while watching Josh out of the corner of my eye. Waiting for a reaction that never came.

"I came to speak with Josh."

Raeford stood beside his son, smiling. He held tight to the bible in one hand, while the other hand draped around Josh's shoulder. "Heard anything about the young man from the college?"

I wanted to hate this man for his smile, his crystal-like eyes, his charm, but I couldn't. Despite being a die-hard bible-thumper, he was nice. A little over-bearing where his family was concerned but he emitted a warm friendliness with strangers that pulled you in, wrapped you in an embrace of graciousness. And he was genuine.

"Unfortunately, it wasn't good news."

His forehead creased with concern, eyes narrowed. "Oh, *no*. I am so sorry to hear that."

Raeford squeezed his son's shoulder, leaning his head into

Josh's. Eyes closed, he recited a prayer with a softer voice than I'd have expected. Josh's lips moved along with his father's, but no sound came out.

As much as Elder Jeremiah would like to think me a heathen for interrupting Emma's baptism, I knew enough protocol to not interrupt a prayer. I stood quietly while Reverend Bloom and Josh prayed for Scott's soul, saying a simple, silent prayer myself.

When they were finished, Raeford hugged Josh tightly. "I'm so sorry, son. I know he was a friend."

Josh jerked his head in a rapid nod and pulled away from his father. "I need to get back to work."

Before I could say anything, Josh pushed by me and disappeared back into the store. I watched the heavy door close, feeling shut out in more ways than one.

"Do they know how it happened?" Raeford asked.

I shook my head. "No. We'll know more after the autopsy."

Raeford stroked the cover of his bible slowly, running his fingers across the gold lettering as if reading braille. More out of habit than with purpose, it seemed to bring comfort. "I really am sorry. I feel for his family."

"I can't imagine the pain of losing a child."

He offered a sad smile and I wondered if he knew the experience first-hand. "Are you in a hurry?"

The question caught me off guard. It was Josh I wanted to spend more time with, but maybe his father held answers Josh didn't. "I can spare a few minutes."

"Walk with me?" He cocked his head to the side and smiled.

We strolled across the parking lot toward the white, clapboard building. The building housing the Higher Heavens Holiness Church looked more like an old deserted hardware store than a church.

Inside, rows of folding metal chairs stood on badly worn carpet like sentries waiting for direction. The pulpit was nothing more than a raised platform with a simple wooden podium in the center. A cross made of sturdy tree limbs hung on the front of the stand, wrapped together with rope, the ends pointed and sharp. Cheaply framed pictures of Jesus at the cross, Jesus walking on water, Jesus and the children, looked like something out of a 1960's Sunday School class.

Raeford carefully watched me take it all in. He ushered me to the front row of chairs and motioned me to sit, taking the seat beside. "We're a simple church, Miss. Logan. We believe in the Word. Plain and simple."

He pointed to the picture of Jesus surrounded by children. "It's an old saying but our children really are our future. We have to raise them right."

Part of me wanted to ask him to define *right*. The other part kept quiet, more interested in where the conversation was headed than definitions.

"This young man, the boy that died—was he a child of God?"

My insides knotted as my discomfort rose. Was it sad that I had no idea how to answer? Scott worked for me, yet I knew very little about him. But like his sexual preference, his religious preference wasn't my concern. I answered as honestly as I could. "I didn't know him well enough to know whether he was or not."

Raeford slowly nodded in that understanding way great advisors do. "I understand. Sometimes we find we don't know people as well as we think we do. Well, let's hope for his sake, and his parents, that he was."

That fire-and-brimstone preacher I'd met on my first visit

had given me chills. This man, quiet and reflective, emitted a comfort I found strange, yet I was curious to continue the conversation. "I'm afraid his parents are going to take it very hard."

"I imagine so. Losing a child is devastating. It's so easy to blame God. To question why. People don't seem to do that as much when the elderly die. You ever notice that?"

I'd never thought about it but he was right. The death of a parent or a grandparent fell into the natural order of things. You didn't question why; you just accepted it. "I guess it's because the death of a child just doesn't feel natural."

He nodded slowly then his soft smile faded into pursed lips. "I suppose you're right. With what Josh told me about the young man, I just hope he set himself right with the Lord before his untimely death."

Set himself *right?* "What did Josh tell you?"

Raeford stood and moved along the row of metal seats, straightening the hymnals lying in the chairs. "Oh, you know, Miss Logan. He was a deeply troubled young man."

Not the Scott Curry I knew. "Troubled how?"

Raeford stopped his nervous work and stared at me, gaging my beliefs perhaps. "He spoke to Joshua of hurting himself. Joshua asked me what to do."

That wasn't what Josh had told me. Not exactly, anyway. Why would Josh hide that when I remember asking him, specifically, if he thought Scott might have hurt himself?

Raeford walked to the make-shift pulpit and straightened the wooden cross, although it didn't need it. "Suicide's a sin, Miss Logan. Many religions tend to overlook that. Do you think taking one's own life is a sin?"

"It doesn't matter what I believe, Reverend Bloom. It

doesn't change the fact a young man is dead. That's the tragedy."

He was slow to nod, and I accepted it as more an acknowledgement than agreement. "You don't think knowing whether he's in heaven or hell matters?"

"Not as much as the fact that he's no longer *here*."

He flinched as if I'd punched him in the gut. He then sucked in a deep, chest-expanding breath and recovered. "What about you, Miss Logan? Are you going to heaven when you pass on? Or are you going to burn in hell?"

I didn't try to suppress a chuckle. "See, that's where mainstream religion and I differ."

He smiled with his whole face, his eyes sparkling like the sun glistening off water. "So you don't really know yourself, do you?"

My eyes narrowed with focus as I tried to figure this man out. "I know."

"Do you?"

Was he mocking me, or trying to save my soul? "Reverend Bloom, with all due respect—my salvation is not what I came here to talk about. A young man who worked for me is dead and I'm trying to understand why. That's all."

He nodded then rejoined me in the first row of chairs. "I understand. Would you be my honored guest this Sunday at morning service? It might help *you* understand better."

Understand *what?*

CHAPTER 20

Scott Curry did not commit suicide. I was certain of that. He wouldn't have left Boone. It was after five when I made it back into town. After calling Doretha to check on the kids, I drove straight to the office. Quinn was still there, finishing up his article on Mary's zoning issue. Nola was long gone, having left a stack of messages on my desk.

I dropped my bag beside my desk. "Any coffee?" I asked Quinn.

He bobbed his head toward the break room. "Just made a pot."

I fixed a cup then brought it back to my desk and started rifling through the messages. Quinn stopped pecking at his keyboard. "I heard about Scott. I'm sorry."

I sat aside the messages requesting free advertising and sighed heavily. "How'd you hear about it? And *what* have you heard?"

Quinn swiveled in his seat, facing me. He laced his fingers behind his head and grinned. "You know how word spreads around here. The only reason we need a newspaper is to clear up the rumors and actually report the facts."

I was too tired to argue. Besides, he was right. "So what are they saying?"

"Not much really. Just that his body was found." Quinn then sprang forward in his seat, propping his elbows on his knees. "Oh! I forgot—the real buzz was who found him and how. Keeper using more of Mary's witchcraft."

I scoffed. "He used dousing rods. It's not witchcraft. Which reminds me, how's the story on the granny women coming?"

"Wrapping it up. I would like to get a quote from Fletcher Hanson, or his mom on why they went to Mary in the first place."

I jumped at the chance, a rush of new adrenaline fueling the leap. "Oh—I want to go with you. But don't tell him I'm coming."

Quinn cocked a brow and frowned. "So we're doing an ambush interview?"

The truth bit at my conscience but I couldn't deny the accusation. "Sort of," I said in a low voice.

He frowned even more. "*Ava*. I know you're the boss, but—"

"There's a possibility he knows something about Scott's death."

Quinn glared at me, his expression morphing from suspicion to confusion. "Seriously?"

I pulled my chair closer to his and sat down then filled him in on everything I'd learned. "If Fletcher and his cousin were in the woods at that time, they may have seen something, or they may be responsible, who knows."

"Do you think these kids are capable of killing a person? I mean an animal's one thing."

"Who knows. It might have been an accident, or maybe they just witnessed something that could help. Or they might honestly not know a thing. Either way, it's worth talking to them again. Have you talked to Fletcher at all?"

He nodded. "Briefly. I had some questions about the side effects of Mary's tonic."

Side effects the idiot kid probably brought on himself. "I'm surprised his dad's letting you talk to him."

Quinn shrugged. "He's a lawyer so he set some ground rules. Besides, he's on a major P.R. campaign. You know, trying to raise some support for his *cause*."

I pushed my chair back to my desk then lifted my bag. "His *cause* being to ruin Mary McCarter," I grumbled. "Text me when you set something up. I'm going to the sheriff's office to see what's new."

I left the paper and drove the mile and half down Main Street to Grayson's office. His car was still in the parking lot, along with the Curry's family sedan. My heart sank as my mind scrambled for what to say. I wasn't expecting them to be here.

Inside, an eerie quietness enveloped the lobby. Even my rubber-soled shoes seemed loud against the tile. Detective Steve Sullivan came out into the hallway from Grayson's office. He fiddled with a set of keys then locked the door behind me "We are officially closed, you know."

I really disliked him. "Are they in Grayson's office?"

"It's never easy doing this part." He slipped the keys back into his pocket.

I followed him down the hall, hesitating outside the door. "Maybe I should just wait out here for a few minutes."

"Suit yourself." He shrugged then disappeared inside the office.

I leaned against the opposite wall going over in my mind what I'd say to Will and Lisa, and Sara. Or questioned if I should say anything at all. Would they find comfort in the silence?

Would they understand? A few minutes later, Sara emerged, red-eyed and breathing heavy. She jerked the door closed behind her.

We stared at each other, neither saying anything for a long while. Finally, she wiped tears from her face and sniffled. "I'm sorry. I just had to get out of there."

I nodded. "You don't have to apologize, Sara."

"The sheriff said they won't know how he died until tomorrow. Maybe not even then."

Making a call on cause of death had no room for errors. It was the difference between a criminal case or a case of natural death. "They have to be thorough."

She sniffled again. "Were you there when they found his body?"

Not knowing what Grayson had told them, I hesitated in saying too much. "Yes."

Sara wrapped her arms around herself like she was holding herself together. Maybe she was. "What do you think it was? I mean, was he shot? Did he fall and hit his head? There had to be some indication of what happened."

I got it. I got the desire to know. The need for an answer. I, too, was searching. "Unfortunately, in situations like this, there's always more questions than answers."

She guffawed. "That's not going to go over very well with my dad."

"I'm sure this is going to be very hard on your parents, and you too, for a long time to come."

Tears cascaded down her cheeks as she struggled with a sob. "He was so happy."

My heart crumbled for her and her parents. I choked back my own tears. "Sara—I am *so* sorry. I wish there was something

I could do to help."

She battled back a deluge, lips quivering. "Just find out what happened to my brother."

The door to Grayson's office opened. I wanted to see him, to feel his strength and calm reserve. But did it make me a bad person to want to run and hide from Will and Lisa Curry? I didn't want to face grieving parents.

Grayson, Sullivan, and the Currys emerged a moment later. Will and Lisa clung to one another, the shell shock still crudely painted on their faces. Sullivan escorted them to the front door. Sara followed then, at the door, turned and gazed at me through red, swollen eyes.

"You said you wished there was something you could do. Find out what happened to my brother."

CHAPTER 21

Ivy played in the floor of the sunroom with her babies while Grayson and I watched from the sofa. She lovingly stroked one's knotted hair then tossed her aside and moved on to the next one. Wouldn't it be wonderful if we all could move on that easily? The memory of Lisa and Will Curry's shell-shocked faces would be with me for a long time. And as her brother's confidant, Sara was forever burdened with knowledge she couldn't, or wouldn't, betray.

Grayson had come home with me, following behind in his own car, after locking up the office, each of us still quiet from the experience with the Currys. Locked somewhere in our own minds, processing their grief. My mind raced with questions to ask him, yet all I could do was watch Ivy play. She wasn't biologically mine, but I don't think I could survive if something happened to her. Or Cole and Emma for that matter. I wondered if Cole and Emma shared secrets like Scott and Sara had? I hoped they never felt the need to keep things from me, but they were kids, I knew there was stuff they didn't want their mother to know. As long as they turned to one another instead of holding on to it by themselves, I was okay with the secrets they kept. Within reason.

Emma came into the sunroom and wedged herself between Grayson and the arm of the sofa. "Mom told me about Scott Curry. Do you suspect foul play?"

Grayson looked at me then scooted over to give Emma more room. "Uh...no. Not at this point."

"I guess you have to wait for the autopsy results. Right?"

Again, Grayson glanced at me before answering. "Yeah. Right."

"Emma's developed an interest in forensic biology," I explained.

"You know...decomp." She stared at Grayson, blank-faced, like it was a natural thing for a twelve-year-old to be curious about a decaying body.

"Oh. Okay. Well, it is a growing field."

I put a halt to the conversation, hoping to discourage her interest in Scott's death. "Would you mind taking Ivy upstairs and getting her ready for bed?"

No hesitation, no grumbling. I couldn't ask for a better kid. "Come on Squirt. Bath time."

Ivy tossed her baby doll and shot up, eager for her bath. Emma hurried to catch her before she made it to the stairs.

"Forensic biology, huh?" Grayson pulled me to him and wrapped me in a tight embrace. His lips found mine in a soft, sweet kiss.

I settled against him, feeling every steady breath. "Can you stay tonight?"

Surprised, he turned and stared at me. We'd made a pact early in our relationship that he wouldn't spend the night while the kids were home. I farmed them off on Doretha when the hormones raged. It might have been hypocritical, but I wasn't comfortable with my kids seeing me with the "just-had-sex afterglow."

He gently tucked my hair behind my ear. "Are you sure?"

I snuggled into him. "I think so. I just don't want to sleep alone tonight."

His lips brushed my forehead. "I'm sorry about Scott."

I let his condolences sink in a moment then sat up and faced him. "Quinn saw Scott at a gay nightclub in Johnson City last weekend. Do you think..."

"But he was involved with this Josh guy, right?"

"From what I've learned from Sara, yes. But...Josh was definitely upset when I told him so there was *something* there. I'm just not sure what exactly."

I told him all about Raeford Bloom and the Higher Heavens Holiness Church. About how it was almost impossible to talk to Josh alone.

I got up from the sofa and started putting away Ivy's toys. "Josh is very quiet and reserved. Almost...awkward."

"Is he like that when his father's not around?"

"It's hard to say. I haven't had much of a chance to talk to him by himself. His father is a very dominating presence." I dropped the alphabet blocks into their plastic container then tossed it in the fairy-covered toy box.

"Did anyone at school know about their relationship?"

"I don't think so. I don't think either one of them is out, so to say."

"What about this bar Quinn saw Scott at?"

I picked up a baby doll with matted hair then plopped on the sofa beside Grayson. "Quinn said it's an underground type thing. He said he didn't think Scott left with anyone, though."

The doll's eyes were the same startling blue as Raeford

Bloom's. Like having chills when you're running a fever, how could something so warm be so cold? I put the doll aside, suddenly creeped out by the fake eyes.

"Can you ask Quinn the name of the bar? Whether he left with anyone or not, it still might be helpful. The more we know about his whereabouts, the better."

My mind flashed a vision of Scott's body, his arms and hands. Scratched and bruised. Like he'd been fighting for his life. "Do you know the cause of death yet?"

"There was some trauma but nothing obvious like a gunshot, although he had some puncture wounds. There was definitely an altercation of some sort. I don't think he died there, though."

"Why?"

"The toes and topsides of his boots were caked with dirt and debris."

"Consistent with being dragged," I said quietly. "And then they covered the body with leaves."

Were they lovingly burying him, or concealing his body?

Emma came back in the room and I was glad I had spoken quietly. She sat on the floor in front of the sofa, knees up, eager for knowledge. "How long does an autopsy take?"

Grayson looked to me for help. I dodged the conversation, hopping up to check on my youngest daughter. "Is Ivy in bed?"

"Oh, yeah. She's waiting on her story."

I hated to desert Grayson but figured if anyone could handle that line of questioning, he could. Just as I reached the door, Emma added, "oh yeah, she's in your bed."

I whirled around and glared at her then looked at Grayson with panic. His usually calm expression was riddled with the same panic I felt. Hurrying up the stairs, sure enough, I found the wide-awake tot in my bed.

"Hey, baby," I cooed. "Let's go to your room and pick out a book."

She giggled and leapt into my arms. I buried my face in her scent, baby fresh and full of sweetness. No decaying bodies, no autopsies. In her room, she crawled into her toddler bed and snuggled underneath her purple and green fairy comforter. I sat on the side of her tiny mattress, wedging myself beside the plastic arm rail and read from her favorite fairy book.

Three stories later, her eyes fluttered shut. I clicked off her lamp and tiptoed out to the hallway where Finn waited at the top of the stairs. Cole's door was cracked so I peeked in. Surprisingly, he was already asleep with his cell phone resting loosely in his outstretched hand. I carefully took it and glanced at the face. The call was still connected to Paisley although the only sound coming from it was light, steady breathing. A smile tickled my lips as I quietly disconnected the call then put the phone on its charger. She was a sweet girl. I'd hate to have to kill her if she broke my son's heart.

I closed his door on my way out, meeting Emma in the hallway. "G'night," she said then kissed me on the cheek.

"Goodnight, Sweetheart." I returned her kiss then followed with a tight hug.

She disappeared into her own room and closed the door. An hour later, Grayson and I did the same.

CHAPTER 22

The next day, a thundering beat pulsated through the expensive speakers in Quinn's Jeep. Top down, wind brushing our hair. The only thing missing was salt air and the roar of the waves. Instead, we climbed higher into the mountains with each winding road. Fletcher Hanson lived with his parents on the outskirts of Jackson Creek in an expansive house straight out of a design magazine.

Quinn slowed to round a sharp curve. "I hope he don't freak out when he sees you with me."

"Gee, thanks." I made an attempt with one hand to keep my hair out of my eyes while holding on to the door handle with the other.

Quinn burst out laughing then cut a glance in my direction. "You don't really think he's going to be glad to see you, do you?"

My gut tightened as he slid the Jeep into the last curve before the Hanson residence. "Probably not." There were certain aspects of my job I couldn't take personally no matter how badly they stung.

Quinn turned onto the paved driveway that snaked through a forest of pines. The house sat on a precipice overlooking

Jackson Creek down below. A multi-level deck jutting from the back of the house provided a breathtaking view of the river and blue-tinged hills beyond. White mountain laurel grew in clusters along the cobblestone walkway leading to the double oak doors gracing the front.

Quinn offered a low whistle, clearly impressed with the Hanson's homestead. "*Jesus*," he whispered. "Makes my apartment look like a dorm room."

"Well his daddy is an attorney."

How unfortunate for Mary. In Appalachia, most people settled differences amongst themselves, often with some encouragement, or discouragement, from law enforcement. Sometimes with shotguns. But we seldom needed litigation lawyers.

"You did make sure a parent would be here, didn't you?" I said. Last thing I needed was Carlyle Hanson coming after me.

"His mom's supposed to be here."

Quinn knocked on the heavy front door, I hung out behind him and leaned against the wrought iron porch railing. Maybe out of guilt. I wasn't an aggressive journalist by nature. I knew my strengths and weaknesses. Truth be known, I was a much better feature writer than investigative reporter.

As Fletcher opened the door his expression went from a teenager without a clue to panic. "You didn't tell me she was coming."

"It's okay. She's just here to do an employee evaluation. I'm due a raise."

The kid eyed me but finally opened the door further for us both to enter. The foyer was the size of Scott's entire apartment. Yet all the money in the world couldn't stop Fletcher's nose bleeds. The Hansons resorted to a granny witch and her free homemade remedies, then turned against her when they screwed it up.

We followed Fletcher into the family room. Professionally decorated with soft leather furniture and original artwork, the room belonged in a design magazine. What did Carlyle Hanson hope to gain by harassing Mary? It couldn't be money.

Quinn settled into the sofa. "So your dad's not here?"

Fletcher straddled an ottoman and laid his cell phone to the side. "No, he's working."

"But your mom's here, right?" Quinn cocked an eyebrow.

Fletcher drummed the ottoman with his short, stubby fingers. "Um, she's running some errands."

"When we set up the interview, your mom said she was going to be here."

"She'll be back. She just ran to the store."

Fletcher Hanson needed to practice his lying skills. My own son Cole had turned lying into an art, so I had a keen eye for falsehoods. Maybe Fletcher lied to his parents better than he lied to us?

Quinn eyed the kid with as much suspicion as I had. He took his notebook out of his pocket then flipped to a blank page. "I wanted to follow up with you about the side effects of the tonic Mary McCarter gave you. Can you tell me about the side effects?"

I didn't like the idea of casting blame on Mary but was bound by ethics to publish the truth, too. I strolled over to the floor-to-ceiling bookcase and pretended to study the titles. Hopefully, if I wasn't standing there staring at him, Fletcher might open up more.

"I threw up a lot and I had a really bad headache."

Quinn made a note then asked, "and you're sure it came

from Mary's tonic?"

Fletcher slowly shrugged. "I guess. I mean...like I wasn't taking anything else."

"And what was it Mary gave you?"

He shrugged again. "I don't know. Some hocus pocus potion or something."

Dumbass didn't even know what he'd taken. "It was Cardinal Flower. And it's toxic if you take too much of it. Did you take too much of it?"

The kid bowed up like a rooster. "I just took what I was supposed to. What she told momma to give me."

I joined Quinn on the sofa and sat on the edge, hands propped on my knees. "So, your mom gave it to you? Every dose?"

Fletcher stared at me, dumbfounded. I wished the thoughts crashing through his brain at that moment were audible. "Yeah...I mean...I guess."

"Do you still have the bottle?"

He blinked several times before answering. "Um...I think we've still got it."

"Would you mind checking? I'd like to smell it. Sometimes that stuff can sour."

It took him a moment, but he finally rose. Without his phone, which meant he wasn't going to run call his cousin for advice. "I'll go get it."

Once he disappeared, Quinn leaned toward me. He spoke between his teeth. Whether out of anger or if he was trying to be quiet, I didn't know. "What are you doing?"

"Mary said she told them it could be toxic if he took too much."

His brows knitted with suspicion. "So you think he took too

much?"

"Maybe. If he didn't follow the directions, that would release Mary of liability."

Quinn did a poor job of suppressing a chuckle. And it wasn't a pleasant chuckle. "Are we here for an interview about granny women or to prove Mary's innocence?"

That stung more than I'd anticipated. As a boss, a friend, and a reporter, that one bit me. "Maybe the interview will prove her innocence?"

Fletcher returned carrying a cobalt blue bottle. The same vintage glass that lined Mary's kitchen shelves. He handed me the bottle then reclaimed the ottoman. I twisted the top off and took a whiff. It wasn't the smell I was after; the bottle was close to empty. A handwritten label attached to the outside with tape gave the date, the contents, and the dosage. I backtracked on a mental calendar to gage the timeframe.

"And when did you end up in the hospital?"

"It was sometime during Easter break. I remember we were out of school."

"Did you take anymore after that?"

He shook his head. If this kid had gone to the hospital during Easter break, and hadn't taken anymore since then, he nearly emptied the bottle in a week.

"Fletcher–if you haven't taken anymore since you got sick, then you took more than you were supposed to. *Way* more."

He shifted his weight and glanced at his phone. "I just took what momma gave me."

Quinn sat up and leaned away from the back of the sofa. "Sounds reasonable. We'll just confirm with your mom when she gets back."

Fletcher's eyes darted back and forth between me and

Quinn. His discomfort was rising. "Um...I don't know when she'll be back."

"You said earlier she had just run to the store," I reminded him.

"Yeah...um. She'll probably be home any minute." He glanced at his phone again, nearing panic mode. I suspected the kid was itching to call Troy.

I turned the bottle over in my hand, contemplating my next move. I wanted so bad to connect the kid with what happened to Scott, but this was Quinn's story about granny women. It wasn't the place or time to bring up a dead cat.

"Fletcher—you know, not only is this stuff toxic when you take too much, it can also kinda get you high. Is that what you were trying to do?" I offered my best understanding mother smile.

He didn't say anything. His eyes darted back and forth between me and Quinn. "No. I didn't try to get *high*. I don't do stuff like that. If I wanted to get high, I'd raid my mom's personal pharmacy."

There are probably no truer words than those spoken from a child. I came close to believing him. I softened my voice and said, "I keep going back to the fact the bottle is almost empty."

A trickle of blood escaped from his right nostril. He brushed it away with the back of his hand then stared at the translucent smear. "I think it's time for y'all to leave."

I reached over and took Quinn's notebook, closed it then sat it to the side. "We're off the record now. Nothing you tell us is going to be used in print."

I knew I was dancing out on a limb with nothing more than a hope and a prayer. And no safety net below. I hoped Quinn would forgive me for trampling all over his story. "Fletcher, you want to tell us what really happened?"

Another trickle of blood. Followed by another. Then a steady stream. He pinched his nostrils together, but the blood kept coming. Now gushing.

I grabbed a box of tissue from the side table and leapt up, rushing to him. Cole'd had one nose bleed in his lifetime, and it stopped as quickly as it had started. This was a rushing crimson-colored river. Quinn jumped in to help, grabbing tissue out of the box and holding them against Fletcher's nose.

"What do you need? Towels? Gauze?" My pulse came rapid-fire. I cursed myself for not knowing what to do.

"Gauze. Kitchen cabinet. By the sink," he muttered, his words clipped.

I left Quinn with Fletcher and dashed to the kitchen, guessing it was in the back of the house. Any other time I would have admired the cabinetry and gourmet cooking area, but now, I was too busy slinging open cabinet doors.

Near the sink. Which side? Open, slam shut, move to the next one. Open, slam shut, repeat. Open...my heart stalled. First aid supplies lined the bottom shelf while prescription bottles too many to count filled the second shelf. I stared at them for a minute, briefly scanning the labels. Anxiety. Depression. Pain. More pain. Sleep. ADHD. More pain. Some of them were for Sandra Hanson, others were different names. Some half full, others only a few pills left.

"Ava," Quinn yelled.

I hurriedly gathered a roll of gauze, a box of nasal plugs, and a box of BloodStop and ran back to the living room. Quinn's hands looked like he'd fallen into a wood chipper.

I rattled off the supplies and asked Fletcher what we needed to do.

"BloodStop," he gurgled.

I tore open a pack and handed it to him, watching him twist the patch into a small cylinder. While he stuffed it up his left nostril, I opened another pack. He did the same to the right side.

A few minutes ago, I wanted to give this kid a talking to. Now I felt sorry for him. If his nose bleeds were this bad, the guy went around school looking like an extra in a slasher movie.

"What else can I do?" I said.

"Get me a wet dish towel from the kitchen."

I headed that way and Quinn followed, anxious to dump all the bloody tissue and wash his hands. When we were alone in the kitchen, he spoke in a quiet voice, "*Damn*—I've never seen that much blood from a nose bleed."

Quinn scrubbed away the evidence over the sink. When he finished, I held a towel under the water. "Take a look in the cabinet on the right," I whispered.

After he dried his hands, he nudged the door open then emitted a low whistle. "Holy crap. That's a lot of meds."

"Easy pickin's too."

CHAPTER 23

I carried the towel to Fletcher and fought the urge to clean his face myself. The mother in me. I wanted to scrub away the crusty, red splotches. Instead, I handed him the towel then returned to the sofa. No matter how hard I tried, I couldn't push away the thought he was involved in something horrible on Spearhead Mountain. Whether It was Fletcher, or Troy or Austin who caused the McCarter cat's death. Fletcher was there. He was an accessory and no matter how sorry I felt for him at the moment, I couldn't forget that.

Luckily, Quinn reminded us of why we were there. "Fletcher, I'm not prying into your family life but there was a ton of meds in that cabinet. Something going on you need to talk about?"

He sounded like a high school guidance counselor. Much more empathetic than me. I said nothing and let him take the lead.

Fletcher continued washing blood from his face, his movement much slower, more thoughtful. Thinking hard on how much to reveal about his family.

Quinn said, "My mother was an alcoholic. I remember in

school my friends used to like coming to my house because there was all the booze you could ever want. That kitchen cabinet reminded me of that. Just pill form instead of liquid."

Fletcher shifted his weight on the ottoman. His expression showed a man/child on the verge of tears. I had to look away to remember what he'd been a part of. The pain he'd inflicted on two people very dear to me hurt more than this kid's problematic home life

With the bleeding stopped, Fletcher removed the nasal plugs. He stared at the bloody stoppers like they held a secret. "My mom had knee surgery awhile back. She also has migraines."

I'd heard this story so many times, I could repeat it verbatim. Jessica Blevins, Sharon Hanson and a thousand other addicts just like them faded into the mountainside. They crept into the landscape like a toxin, devouring lives as they went along with no regard for others. It happened so frequent now, we'd grown immune to the destruction. Or either we just looked the other way.

Quinn said, "All the pills...are they your mom's?"

Fletcher nodded. I stared at a tiny splotch of blood stuck to his cheek. How many times had Sharon doctored his skinned knees, kissed his boo-boos? Wiped away the blood from a lifetime of nose bleeds?

Rustling in the kitchen grabbed my attention. Quinn and I both jerked our heads up then looked at one another. A woman's voice called for Fletcher then grew louder as it came our way. A moment later, Sharon Hanson stood at the edge of the living room staring at the three of us, her mouth hanging open.

"*Fuck*. That was today, wasn't it." Her words were slurred. Focus dilated.

"Mom...." Fletcher rolled his eyes.

She was close to forty and looked every day of it. Too many days in the tanning bed produced leather, not the soft bronzed glow she'd probably hoped for. Bleached blonde hair tucked into a messy bun, every other manicured nail painted bright pink, the others deep lavender.

"I'm sorry, y'all. I totally forgot you wanted to talk to Fletch about..." She stopped completely, struggling to regain her train of thought.

"The tonic," Quinn said.

Sharon slapped her hand at the air like she had just remembered. "That's right. That shit that woman gave my son. Almost killed him."

I bit my tongue. Between her and Jessica Blevins, these kids didn't stand a chance.

"Yeah, that so-called medicine put him in the hospital." Sharon finally took a hard look at her son then her eyes flew wide open. She jerked the towel away from him and stabbed at the remaining blood speck on his cheek "*Jesus*, Fletcher. What the hell happened?"

Fletcher pulled away, pushing her hand aside. "It's okay. It's under control."

She jabbed her finger toward me and Quinn. "You see what that crap did to him? The bleeds weren't this bad before he started taking that mess."

Fletcher's shoulders dropped, weighed down by embarrassment. He jerked the towel away from her and nervously twisted it into knots. "Mom, stop. Just stop the whole thing."

Quinn and I threw one another a glance. Neither of us wanted to spoil Fletcher's moment with a barrage of questions.

The truth was slowly creeping out on its own.

Sharon, mouth agape, stumbled over her words. "Fletcher, you need...you need to...your daddy needs to handle this." She turned to me and Quinn, hands spread apologetically. "I'm sorry guys—we're going to have to cut this short. We probably shouldn't be talking to you anyway since there's a lawsuit pending."

A lawsuit? It was supposedly just a zoning issue. Anger flashed through my veins like sparkplugs firing. "Wait a minute. Y'all are suing Mary McCarter?"

Fletcher wrung the towel like he was wringing a wet mop. Lips twitching.

"All that crap she sells is gonna kill somebody someday."

I stood, my nails digging into my palms. "Mary doesn't *sell* anything."

"Whether its sold or its free, the stuff put my kid in the hospital."

"Half the bottle's gone, Sharon. Mary told you it could be toxic if you take too much."

Sharon huffed, jammed her arms across her chest, and rolled her eyes. "You know how kids are. They don't pay attention to instructions."

Fletcher slammed the wash towel on the ottoman and shot up like a bullet. Red-faced and it had nothing to do with the bloody nose. "Stop it," he screamed. "You're not blaming me for this anymore, Mom."

Sharon spun around. "Fletcher—you need to hush."

"No. I won't hush."

I backed away from the two, not wanting to be in the middle of a family squabble more than I already was. Fletcher's eyes were damp while his mother's flamed with fury.

He smacked away a stray tear that had escaped. "You gave me that medicine, mom. You're the one who gave me too much."

Sharon jerked around to me and Quinn. Desperate. Panicked. "He doesn't remember. He was so out of it when they admitted him to the hospital."

"No! Just admit what you did. You even lied about it to Dad."

Like a flashover, Sharon slapped her son with enough force to knock him sideways. Quinn lunged, grabbing Fletcher and pulling him away from his mother. The kid was screaming, swinging wildly. I moved between Sharon and Fletcher and herded her toward the kitchen. Anywhere to separate the two. She raised her hands, ready to shove me backwards then thought better of it. Turning away, she stomped down the hallway toward the kitchen. I looked at Quinn, then followed her.

"He don't know what he's talking about." She grabbed hold of the counter, knuckles white, hands trembling. "That crazy woman nearly killed him."

The only crazy woman involved with this was standing in front of me, grasping at straws as hard she grasped the counter. The reality of the tonic wasn't the only truth I needed. I needed to know what happened on Spearhead mountain. That wouldn't come from a pill-popper but if Fletcher would share his secrets, I'd consider keeping my mouth closed about his mother's.

"I'm going back to the living room. When you no longer want to hit your son, feel free to join us."

I left her standing there, clutching for support she wasn't going to get from me, and went back into the living room. Quinn sat with Fletcher on the sofa, dripping with compassion. They both looked up when I came in. A red welt stretched from

Fletcher's cheek bone to the corner of his eye. The kid looked emotionally and physically beat down.

All I could say at that moment was, "I'm sorry." I sat across from them on the ottoman, stealing glances with Quinn. Poor guy. His story had plunged deep into a gorge. I'd make it up to him somehow.

From the kitchen, the back door slammed hard enough, I flinched. A minute later, a car cranked then tore out of the driveway. I'd deal with the accusations about Mary and that pending lawsuit after I found out what happened to Scott.

I spoke quietly. "Fletcher, let's move past the tonic for a moment. At least the part about how you ended up taking too much. I know you and your cousins were up on Spearhead Mountain a few days ago, around the same time Scott Curry went missing. I also know Troy told Keeper McCarter y'all killed his cat because of the tonic—"

"I didn't kill any cat. That was all Troy." He spat out the words like spitting scalding coffee. A defense mechanism. He gnawed on his bottom lip. Foot began to tap nervously. The physical altercation with his mother, the stress bleed from mine and Quinn's earlier questions, this kid was a cluster of nerve endings on fire.

I hated using the murder of a defenseless pet as a bargaining tool. "We'll deal with Troy later. Tell me everything you saw that day. Minus the cat."

"We didn't see nothing. We were the only ones there. I swear."

"You didn't see *anything* out of the ordinary?"

"Think, Fletcher," Quinn added. "Maybe a vehicle you didn't recognize?"

He shifted around on the sofa. Foot still tapping. "We found a backpack."

My breath stilled for a fraction of a second. "Describe it."

"It was a North Face. Blue and black, maybe. I can't remember exactly."

Scott's was green and black, but it was a North Face. Too much of a coincidence to let it go. "Where'd you see it?"

"It was a little ways off the trail. Not far from where Troy...you know."

Broke a cat's neck? I took a breath before continuing. "Did you do anything with the backpack?"

"We went through it. Wasn't much in it but hiking stuff and a bunch of papers."

The only paper we found was a trail map. "What kind of papers?"

Fletcher shrugged. The tapping had stopped but he still looked edgy. "Weird shit. About poison and stuff."

That made no sense. There were no papers in the backpack. "What did you do with them?"

He shrugged again. "I don't know. Troy just threw 'em down, I guess."

"And what did you do with the backpack?"

"Austin wanted to see if the waterproof case worked so we took it down to the river. He was goin' to just hold it under and it started floating away from him. Retard tried chasing it down then we all just watched it float down river."

And these brainiacs called Keeper names? "You said the backpack was off the trail a little ways. How far was that from where Troy killed the cat?"

Another shrug. "Twenty, thirty feet maybe. It was right around there."

Quinn threw me a glance as he started the jeep. "Spearhead

Mountain?"

"Got your hiking shoes on?"

He didn't but his high-dollar sneakers would work just fine. I kept a pair of hikers in the Tahoe for emergencies, but we weren't in my car, and I was in too much of a hurry to swing by the office. Loafers would have to do.

I pulled my hair into a clip to avoid the whipping wind of driving with the top down. By my calculations, we were twenty minutes out.

"You know where we're going when we get there?"

I knew. The spot where Scott's body was found was seared into my memory. "There's a small parking lot at the trail head. The actual location's about a mile in, a little ways off the trail."

My mind raced as fast as the Jeep rounded the bends in the road. Never slowing down, prepared for a crash. "Hey, Quinn—" I spoke over the rush of the wind, "what was the name of that bar you saw Scott at?"

"Shenanigans." He looked over at me, brows knitted. "I only saw him there once. And he didn't leave with anyone. At least I don't think he did."

"But you're not sure?"

"I suppose he could have met someone in the parking lot. They hit it off. Who knows."

I pulled out my phone and opened the picture of Scott and Josh then quickly showed it to Quinn. "Ever see him before?"

He stole a glance then shook his head. "No, and he's not really a bar-looking kinda guy."

I studied the picture, staring hard into Joshua Bloom's eyes. There was something there I couldn't put my finger on. Josh's eyes weren't as receptive as his father's, but neither were they darkly suspicious. "What's your story, Josh?" I mumbled then texted the name of the bar to Grayson.

Quinn said, "Were they involved?"

That was the question of the day. "Depends on who you ask." I explained what Sara had told me about the relationship, and about Josh's demeanor when I told him about Scott's death.

"That's tough. Being involved with someone and something bad happens and you can't acknowledge it."

"Are you speaking from personal experience?"

He shot me a look and smiled softly. "Yes."

Quinn offered nothing else and I didn't want to pry. He would tell me sooner or later. I pointed ahead. "Follow the switchback and the parking lot is on the right."

He turned onto Crest View Road then pulled into the lot. There were no other cars there. We hurried into the woods, following the trail. About a mile in, we found the spot where Scott's body was found. A piece of torn crime scene tape was still wrapped about the branch of a dogwood, flapping like a yellow caution flag. The sheriff's department had cleared the scene. There was no need for the reminder. I ripped it down and stuffed it in my pocket.

Quinn stood staring at the ground. "What exactly am I supposed to be looking for?"

"Papers." I pushed dirt around with the toe of my shoe. "Fletcher said they found the backpack not far from where the body was found, so we should be in the general vicinity. Look for anything that doesn't belong."

He turned in one direction, and I went the other. The marks where Scott's body had been dragged looked like plow lines in the dirt, partially hidden beneath fallen leaves. I followed along until the lines faded back into the earth. Every broken branch, crushed twigs, could indicate a struggle. Leaves ripped from branches, blood spatter? I backtracked until I stood at the exact spot where he was found. The only crushed leaves were in the slight indention where his body had met the ground. My focus went to several dark spots on a cluster of leaves. I stooped, lightly touching a large leaf. My fingertips were smudged with an oily sheen. Grayson had said Scott's clothes had trace amounts of some kind of grease. Was it already here and he was dragged through it?

I thought of Keeper's bicycle and its old pedals and brakes. But the day Grayson and I ran into him in the woods, his bike had been in the parking lot.

Quinn called, jerking me out of my trance. "Hey, Ava...found something."

I hurried over to him. Pine branches whipped across my face, tore at my arms. "What have you got?"

Several pieces of discarded paper littered a thicket. We gathered up as much as we could then rifled through them. Most were printed pages from websites. The CDC, Mayo Clinic, Poison Control...although the websites were different, the subject was the same. Variations of poison.

My mind raced back to the books on Scott's kitchen table. I couldn't remember the exact title but one had something to do with poison. Poison. Snakes. And religion.

Higher Heavens Holiness Church. The bible verse printed on the tract. Mark 16:17-18

"Oh my God," I mumbled. "It's a snake handling church."

Quinn stared at me, brows knitted. "What is?"

"Joshua Bloom's church. I bet that's what Scott was researching."

Quinn glanced around the woods like he fully expected something to jump out at us. "Those churches really exist?"

"Oh yeah. Deep in the hills." My chest thumped with adrenaline as thoughts came together. "Quinn—that pile of dead snakes. Where did Jenkins Tooley find them?"

He looked around, shoulders lifted in question. "Um...I'm not even sure where *we* are. I know we didn't park in the same parking lot where we are now. I remember that much."

My mind raced with landmarks I knew along the trail. Although the trail was a loop, there was a connector point about a mile north. I'd never come in that way so didn't know if there was a parking lot attached or not. I figured we were about to find out.

Quinn followed me back to the trail then we turned northward. Sunlight broke through the canopy of trees like a spotlight. The strong scent of pine hung heavy in the air. We found the connector and veered off the loop.

"Anything look familiar?" I said.

"Seen one tree, seen them all. I'm not from around here, as you like to remind me."

Any other time, I would have smiled. Now, I just pushed forward.

"Oh, wait—I remember that boulder over there." Quinn stopped and pointed to his right. A mammoth rock jutted from the earth, leading like a ladder up a steep incline. We hurried off the trail to the spot.

I searched the area, looking for anything out of the ordinary. We were far enough off the trail that the dump site was intentional. "This is where Jenkins found the snakes?"

Quinn nodded. "I remember the rock. It was a pile of them dumped right where you're standing."

Jenkins Tooley must have walked off the trail to take care of nature and then stumbled upon the dead snakes. I looked over the tree line, calculating how far the clearing was. "That back parking lot's not that far from here. I bet that's where they came in at."

I led us back to the trail then moved quickly to the connector trailhead. It emptied into a tiny parking lot, gravel, with a dilapidated sign that said Big Rock Trail. So original I almost laughed.

"Is this where you met Jenkins?"

"Yeah. Still don't know why he called the paper before calling the park service."

I did laugh at that one. "The paper is all-knowing. At least everyone thinks we are."

The small lot was in need of a load of fresh gravel and some litter clean up. An empty fast-food bag, a discarded motor oil container, three crushed beer cans, two soda bottles, and a well-worn ball cap marred the already lackluster landscaping.

Although the array of trash irked me, the hat pulled me in. Gray with a forest green "B" on the front. Brighton College? I remembered the girl in the office that showed me to the library – the t-shirt she wore with the school's logo had the same colors.

I picked it up and shook off the dirt. A smudge of dirt clung to the side. I rubbed at the spot and my fingers came away greasy. Much like the leaves back at where Scott's body was found. I spun around and stared at the tossed motor oil container.

It was just like the others in the back of Josh's truck.

That night, armed with my laptop, I hunted down everything I could find on the internet about snake handling churches. Although they were as much a part of Appalachia history as coal mines and moonshine, their existence was cloaked in mystery. I'd grown up surrounded by them—yet could only name a few and they were the ones documentaries focused on. Visitors weren't always welcome. It all made sense now

The practice started decades ago, near the turn of the century, when a Church of God preacher named George Went Hensley began pounding the pulpit with literal interpretation of the book of Mark, chapter 16, verse 18. *"They shall take up serpents; and if they drink any deadly thing, it shall not hurt them; they shall lay hands on the sick, and they shall recover"*

Based out of a little town in southeastern Tennessee called Grasshopper Valley, Hensley left the Church of God after they denounced snake handling. Hensley formed his own body of believers. Around that same time, other serpent-handling believing churches sprang up in Alabama and Georgia. The practice spread throughout the region, reaching deep into the hollers were folks clung to hope of any kind.

Although outlawed even back then in all Appalachian states except West Virginia, the practice remains often overlooked by law enforcement. Easier to look the other way than become involved in a civil suit claiming violation of freedom of religion. They only get involved when a death occurs.

My mind reeled with possibilities. Was Scott killed during a service then dumped because they didn't want to get law enforcement involved? Could the puncture wounds on Scott's body have been from snake bites?

I read further about the churches use of poison, most often strychnine. *"And if they drink any deadly thing, it will not hurt them..."*

The papers Quinn and I had collected from the crime scene, the books at Scott's about poison. I was now convinced the

Bloom's not only knew something about Scott's death, but were involved.

CHAPTER 24

The next morning, sparks bit at my jumpy nerves. Reverend Raeford Bloom had offered an invitation to visit his church, and I was taking him up on it. The kids would listen to Doretha preach today while I would sit in a folding chair and pray Raeford didn't bring out the snakes. My hands shook as I fussed with Ivy's hair, trying my best to wrangle a hair bow into the blonde curls. She fought my efforts with twists and turns, insisting on feeding her baby doll at that moment. Dressed in a yellow plaid sundress, with or without the hair bow, she was such a cute child. At two years old, her baby features were beginning to even out. The chubby cheeks, pouty lips, and lashes women pay big bucks for were still there, but the baby rolls were fading.

Growing impatient, she fussed to go downstairs where Emma waited. Jeremiah would be here soon to pick them up in the church bus. I could have dropped them off at Doretha's on my way to Higher Heavens Holiness Church, but they enjoyed the bus ride.

I snuck a peek in the mirror, hoping I wouldn't stand out in Reverend Bloom's congregation. Navy capris, simple white t-shirt, and casual sandals. A dab of makeup and a sweep of the brush through my hair, and I was ready.

Ivy insisted on being a big girl and walk down the steps herself. She held the banister with one hand, while carrying her baby with the other. Afraid to get too far away from her, I walked beside her, fighting the urge to just whisk her up and be done with it. It took twice as long to get down the steps, but I couldn't carry her all her life.

Cole fed from a cereal bowl the size of a troth at the kitchen table. "What time will y'all be back?" Milk dribbled from his chin and I wondered if I'd truly given birth to him.

I raised a brow, questioning his motives. Not that I didn't trust him. It was a habit. "It'll be later this afternoon. Why?"

"I'm going to Paisley's for a cookout. Her parents invited me over."

Jeremiah honked the bus horn from the driveway, sending Emma scurrying to herd Ivy out the door and Finn into a barking tailspin. Boone had mistakenly made himself at home by now so stood with ears erect watching Finn. The cat didn't seem to mind living with a dog as long as he was fed on a regular basis.

I rushed to give the girls a kiss before they hurried out the door. From the porch, I offered Jeremiah a forced smile and lackluster wave. He did the same minus the smile.

Back inside, Cole stood at the sink rinsing out his bowl. That was a first. And then I remembered he wanted to go to Paisley's. "What time is this cookout you're invited to?"

His face turned hopeful. "Around two. Paisley said she'd come get me."

"Alright. But you have to be home by seven. It is a school night."

To my surprise he pecked me on the cheek. "Thank you. You're the best. I don't care what Emma says."

I couldn't fight the smile playing with my lips as he rushed upstairs. "Lock up when you leave. And take your cell phone with you." My words trailed behind.

I patted Finn's head and stared into those warm golden eyes wondering if I was doing the right thing. I had no business in Raeford Bloom's church, yet it offered the chance to observe father and son in action.

The Bloom's held the key to the mystery surrounding Scott's death. I knew they did.

I gave Finn another pat on the head then headed to church just like any other Sunday morning go-er. Except this was a church far away from the mainstream. A small amount of guilt came with the knowledge I wasn't being one-hundred percent honest with Raeford Bloom. Instinct told me he wasn't being totally honest with me, either.

When I crossed the state line into Virginia, my palms started sweating. A deep breath helped restore the calm and steady my nerves. There was no need to be nervous. It was just a church. With snakes.

Although that part hadn't been confirmed, all signs pointed to that conclusion.

About twenty vehicles crowded around the white building. Most were older models, some in need of new paint or tires. Four-door sedans equaled the number of pickup trucks and SUVs. I parked beside a wood-paneled station wagon straight out of the 1970s. From the sound coming from the church, the service was already underway. A rousing hymn filtered through the old building's crevices then filled the surrounding mountains when I opened the door.

The congregation sang praises loud and proud, hands raised, arms swaying with the spirit. Tambourines clanged and shimmied with jittery rhythm. A man I recognized from the barber shop hurried over to meet me. The surprise in his face wasn't as welcoming as I'd anticipated. His short-sleeve button-down shirt with pearl snaps looked like it belonged with the station wagon parked outside.

If there had been a foyer, he would have herded me into it and away from the service. "Can I help you, missy?"

"Reverend Bloom invited me." I raised my voice to be heard over the music.

He looked back at the pulpit where Raeford stood behind the podium, gazing out over his flock of believers. When Raeford spotted me, he was slow to smile but eventually waved.

I returned the wave then turned to the barber. "I'll just sit back here if that's alright."

He looked at Raeford again then ushered me to an empty chair on the back row. I scooted in past a lady clapping and shouting in glory and took my seat. The barber took his seat on the end, beside the heaven-bound woman. She, like some of the other women, wore a modest, ankle-length skirt and concealing, button-up blouse. Some wore conservative, knee length dresses while the younger ones sported jeans. No one wore make-up. I probably looked like a twenty-dollar whore with even the bare minimal sparingly covering my face. The air in the church was stuffy, filled with sweat, drug store perfume and years-old aftershave. With no air circulating, perspiration trickled down the back of my neck.

After the song was over, the praising continued. Some rose to their feet talking in a different language, speaking in tongues I'd heard about the phenomenon but had never witnessed it.

Words, foreign words, words that made no sense to others recited in a ritualistic-like trance. Sometimes, I understood Doretha when the spirit moved her, but she spoke English or Latin, maybe Hebrew, but it was a real language. This was babble. I didn't want to stare at the worshipers like they were freaks, because they weren't, but I couldn't look away. Totally drawn in. Mesmerized. Not by the holy spirit they summoned, but by the sincerity of their belief. It was pure, honest. It may not have been the same as my own personal beliefs, but it was all consuming. The Holy Spirit or some other entity had filled these people at this moment and it was real.

My eyes landed on Josh and the rest of the Bloom family, front row and center. Josh sat beside his mother with a stoic look on his face. He showed little interest in the service, appearing either bored or angry about being there. I wondered if attending services was mandatory since he was the preacher's son.

Raeford shouted out a verse, jerking my attention away from the tongue talkers. He pounded a fist on the podium and the impact knocked the wooden cross loose. More shouts of praise and arms raised to heaven, while the rockabilly music added to the frenzy. Raeford preached above the music with a rabid fervor. The scene could easily scare a child, yet the few that were there went unfazed by the excitement.

I thought of Emma standing in that river with her muddied gown, and Doretha so filled with the spirit. Despite the rising heat in the church, a chill tickled my spine at the memory of the icy water.

Raeford moved around the pulpit like a dancer, lifting his hands in praise and spouting verse after verse. Stomping his feet, almost jumping in place. Sweat dripped from his forehead and seeped through his shirt. He clapped in rhythm to the music, engulfed in sheer rapture. A wave of confusion washed over me as I felt embarrassed to witness something so personal. In my mind, at least, what should be an intimate moment between oneself and their maker had turned into a spectacle–yet I was the only one watching.

The others, mostly with their eyes closed, were so focused on their own experience, Raeford's sermon was mere background noise.

When the song finally ended, Raeford took a moment to catch his breath. He pulled a handkerchief from his pocket and wiped his face. "Joshua, Roland and Douglas—will you bring in the serpents?"

The two other men leapt up and disappeared through a door behind the pulpit. Josh's mother nudged him until he dragged himself up to follow the other men. This wasn't the same sensitive kid I'd talked with at the grocery store. Anger and resentment bubbled to the surface, showing in his clenched jaw and cold eyes. With the crowd of worshipers captured in a trance-like euphoria, Josh and the other two men re-appeared carrying wooden crates. They stood beside Raeford as he recited scripture from memory.

The tongue talker celebration intensified, and I wanted to look away, but couldn't. I hugged myself tightly, warding off the chill creeping through my body. This wasn't like any service I'd ever witnessed of Doretha's. Even with the river baptisms and bongo playing, this was totally different. Captivating, and frightening at the same time.

As Raeford shouted to heaven, a small group of believers headed down to the pulpit. "They shall take up serpents," Raeford shouted. Sweat poured over his reddened face.

Joshua and the other two men sat the crates on the stage. I knew what was about to happen, yet my heart stopped cold. Someone could easily die here today, in the name of God. I wanted so bad to believe that was what happened to Scott. That his death wasn't through ill intent.

I forced my lungs to push the air out of my chest as Raeford opened one of the crates and removed a timber rattler. He held it up to God as an offering of sorts and recited more scripture as it draped across his arm, tongue flickering, rattle vibrating.

Raeford handed the snake to one of the worshipers who also held it up to heaven. The woman beside him babbled in tongue. Raeford opened the second crate and pulled out a slithering copperhead. The snake stretched out to its full length, taking both of Raeford's hands to hold it. I estimated three-and-half feet, maybe four. People clamored to the pulpit, some singing praises while others spoke in tongue, all eager to hold the snakes. To prove their belief.

Raeford tossed the snake into the crowd and shouted, "It *shall not* hurt them. They *shall lay hands* on the sick. And they *shall recover*." His voice rose with each word until I was certain the force would lift the roof.

The rattler shimmied its rattle while the copperhead lunged for a man's arm but failed to connect. My throat tightened with fear as my heart pounded in my chest. The man smiled triumphantly, praising the almighty then passed the serpent to the man behind him. It wasn't so much about avoiding the bite, as it was avoiding medical attention if it happened.

Josh opened the crate at his feet and didn't wait for his father. He reached in and pulled out another timber rattler, this one longer and thicker and angrier. It came out sounding a warning. Josh held it up over his head like he was declaring victory. He didn't shout or speak in tongue and the look in his eyes was as angry as the rattler's.

His mother rocked back and forth in her seat, holding her hands out in front of her, palms up. Fully engulfed in the spirit. I wanted to shake some sense into her and scream her son was in danger, but then gasped as Josh launched the snake into the crowd. A beefy man with a beard to his chest caught the creature mid-air and yelled, "Glory is the kingdom!"

He was only a few feet away. Close enough I could hear the angry snake's trademark sound over the cacophony. I wanted to run but my feet wouldn't move, my legs wouldn't carry me away from this madness.

All of a sudden, Josh grabbed me by the arm and jerked me toward the door. I stumbled over my own two feet as he hurried outside but he didn't let go. Instead, he dragged me away from the building, shoving me against the Tahoe.

Charcoal-colored clouds filled the sky, suspended over the peaks as if impaled. Fat raindrops fell in prelude to a coming downpour. A crack of thunder ripped through the hills, competing with the heart-thumping music pulsating from the church.

Josh spun around, slapping his hands to his head. "Why are you here?" He shouted. But it wasn't anger that filled his eyes. It was desperation. Tears streamed down his face.

I didn't know what to do. I wanted to reach out to him, but I was paralyzed with fear.

"You have no business here," he stuttered. "Just go back to Jackson Creek and leave us alone."

Rain fell harder now, clinging to my lashes. "Josh—what happened to Scott?"

He didn't say anything and looked back at the church. He

then turned back to me, his eyes filled with resolve. His voice was soft, almost pleading. “Please. Just go home.”

He quickly crossed the parking lot then disappeared back inside the church. I stood there a moment, in the rain, to let my nerves settle then slid into the Tahoe. I wasn’t leaving this parking lot without talking to Raeford or Josh, or both.

CHAPTER 25

I sat in the parking lot and waited for the service to be over. The storm was deafening with thunder exploding like the dynamite used to blow the tops off coal-yielding mountains. Lightening cracked and popped like a pyrotechnical sideshow. Rain fell against the windshield in a hyper staccato rhythm.

The storm went on for close to an hour. The service lasted closer to three. People filed out of the church looking exhausted, spent. For something that was supposed to be uplifting, this service seemed to leave the worshipers drained. But then again, I'd never witnessed a service so physical. They lumbered to their cars, some stepping over the puddles, others splashing right through the rainbow prisms.

I watched Raeford's wife and the two youngest children climb into the wood-paneled station wagon. Susan Bloom sat on the passenger side. A moment later, Josh came out and slid behind the wheel. He threw a cold stare at me then slowly drove away.

I waited until the station wagon was out of sight then rushed to the church. I took a minute to catch my breath and collect my nerves. After a moment, I stepped inside the darkened church. A light in the pulpit highlighted the podium and wooden cross while a white glow flickered behind the partially closed door to the storage room.

I stood at the first row of chairs, hesitant to venture further. "Raeford."

A moment later he stepped out of the storage room. An eastern diamondback draped over his forearm. "Ava. You left early." He smiled as warmly as ever as he came out and joined me.

I eyed the snake cautiously. "I need to talk to you. And Josh."

"He'll be back in a few minutes. He just ran down to the house to gather some supplies." The snake writhed silently across Raeford's outstretched arm, its cold eyes in deep contrast to Raeford's. "How can I help you?"

I wanted to pull from the memory of our first meeting when I didn't trust Raeford Bloom–when I found him more sinister than genuine.

"Did Scott ever visit the church?"

Raeford watched the snake stretch its body toward his neck then allowed it to climb across his shoulder. "Scott was a troubled young man, Ava."

"You didn't answer the question, Raeford."

He laughed then guided the snake back to his arm. "Maybe I should be a politician, huh?"

"Maybe you already are."

He pulled his eyes away from the reptile and stared at me. I'd never felt more vulnerable in my life. My blood ran as cold as the snake's. Raeford's whole face then opened up into a smile. "Politicians, preachers. Just doing our part to help society." He gently placed the reptile in one of the two remaining crates.

"You still haven't answered my question. Did Scott ever attend a service here?"

He lifted the crate and carried it to the storage room then returned a moment later. "Yes. Scott visited the church a time or two." He hoisted the last crate then said, "Come on back. We'll talk about it."

Raeford disappeared again into the back room and I stood frozen in place. Too terrified to move. To scared not to. The answers I sought were in that storage room and despite the fear, I'd find them.

I followed him to the back room where my brain forgot to tell my lungs to breath. Rows of aquariums lined two walls. Ten in all. Ten snakes of various sizes. Raeford carefully lowered the eastern diamondback into one of the glass enclosures then placed a wire mesh covering over the top. He used bungee cords to hold it in place. He stacked the wooden crates in the corner.

I knew enough about snakes to know the ones with diamond-shaped heads were poisonous. And every single one of these snakes were deadly. I couldn't look away from the eyes staring back at me, or the flickering tongues searching for my scent.

My eyes moved from the snakes to the top shelves. Large plastic containers marked with skulls and crossbones sat above the snakes.

Despite the snakes being enclosed, I moved slowly and cautiously. Like approaching an unfamiliar dog. The only thing not moving slowly was my heart. It beat so hard and fast, I wondered if Raeford could hear it.

A copperhead pushed against the wire mesh top covering its glass crate. Instinctively, I backed away from the aquarium, and backed straight into Raeford.

He didn't move. Not even an inch. I jerked around to face him and nearly stumbled backwards at the suddenness of the closeness. He grabbed my arms to steady me. "Careful there."

I eased away from him, away from the awkwardness.

He relaxed and casually leaned against one of the shelves holding the aquariums. "Do the serpents scare you?"

"No. But their venom does."

He let out a quick, sharp laugh. "Oh, Ava. If you believe, if you have faith, there's nothing to fear."

"Have you ever been bitten?"

He raised the left sleeve of his work shirt and pointed to a nice set of fang marks. "I won't lie to you—it hurt."

"The bite or the venom?"

"The bite. Never felt the venom. God doesn't keep us from being bitten. He *does* protect us from the toxins if our belief is strong enough. Is your belief strong enough, Ava?"

"My belief isn't the question. I'm more interested in Scott's."

He nodded, never taking his eyes off of me. "Scott was—"

At that moment, I lost any patience I had with the man. "Yes, I know. He was *troubled.* Did Josh share your ways with Scott, Raeford? Is that why Scott's dead?"

The softness in his face vanished but he didn't answer.

"Scott's body has evidence of snake bites. Did he not have *the faith*?"

His usually startling eyes turned dark, shadowed. "Maybe you better leave now."

"Raeford, I know about Josh and Scott. I know about their relationship."

He was quick to shake his head. "No. There was no relationship. As I said, he was a troubled young man."

The cool persona was slipping and giving way to a worried father. No wonder he was so protective of Josh. He was in denial. "The Scott I knew wasn't troubled. His sister said he was very happy. He told her he'd met someone. That someone was Josh, wasn't it, Raeford?"

Anger flashed in his eyes. He clenched his jaw. "It wasn't *natural.*"

So it was more than a religious experience Scott was referring to when he told Sara he was happy. "Did Josh know how Scott felt?"

Raeford huffed then sucked in a breath. "Of course he knew. It made him very uncomfortable. He didn't know what to do, how to handle it."

"Tell me what happened."

He turned away and fiddled with the top on one of the enclosures, busying himself. "There's nothing to tell. The young man pursued a relationship that wasn't natural. My son's not a homosexual, Ava."

With beliefs entrenched so deep into a religious doctrine, arguing with him about what's wrong and what's right and what falls into a gray area would serve no purpose. Getting to the bottom of why a young man died was my purpose.

"Did Josh share *this*...talking in tongues, and the snake handling with Scott?" I waved my hands around the room at the menagerie. "Did he try to *preach* to him somehow?"

Raeford spun around with a look of total disgust painted over his face. "Share *this*? The talking in tongues, the serpent handling, are *gifts*. Not everyone can understand or appreciate the beauty of the gifts." His voice rose and fell as if he were in the pulpit. He took a step toward me. I could smell his sweat. "I invited you to our service to save your soul, not to criticize how we worship." Anger filled his words and popped from between clenched teeth.

"I'm not criticizing. You're free to worship however you want as long as it doesn't infringe on anyone else's safety." I motioned to the containers of Strychnine on the top shelves. "Venomous snakes, poison—those aren't gifts. That's safety hazards."

"They can be if you don't believe in the Lord God's protection."

"Are you saying Scott didn't believe?"

"Josh said he called us freaks. He called *us* freaks. A man who wants to lay with another man."

He took another step toward me and I took a step backward, suddenly aware I was cornered. Raeford stood between me and the door. "If a man lies with a man as one lies with a woman, both of them have done what is detestable." The glow in his eyes was threatening and for the first time, I wasn't just uneasy, I was afraid of him.

"They must be put to death; their blood on their own heads."

"Raeford—"

"Father?" Josh stood at the door, confusion pulling his mouth into a frown.

Raeford whirled around to face his son. "Joshua. Tell her—tell her what that boy wanted you to do. Tell her the horrible—"

"No!" Josh shouted. "It wasn't horrible. It wasn't ugly. It was wonderful, Father. It was *wonderful.*"

Raeford slapped his son with enough force to knock Josh sideways. His lip bloodied, Josh spit blood then stared at the spatter on the floor. "I *loved* him."

Raeford spat. "Love? That's not love."

"How do you know? Your love is all about force, and fear. You think Mother loves you? She *fears* you."

Raeford threw a closed-fist punch at his son, connecting on his jaw. The force knocked Josh into one of the shelves, sending the aquariums crashing to the ground. Glass shattered and flew like shrapnel. Tiny slivers scattered on the floor, sparkling like jagged jewels as the now free snakes slithered across them. A scream erupted from deep in my lungs as I scrambled to get away. The snakes moved wildly and quickly in all directions. I backed further into the corner, trapped. Frantic, I climbed the shelf, pulling my feet up as high as I could get them.

Josh swung wildly, landing a punch to Raeford's face but Raeford was so much stronger. "Why?" Josh screamed. "Why'd you have to kill him?"

The two men slammed against the other row of glass enclosures, bouncing from one wall to the other. The shelves rattled from the force, toppling the plastic containers to the ground, spilling their contents. Fine, white powder exploded around us. Raeford's right foot came down hard on a massive timber snake, causing the serpent to strike out. Raeford screamed out as it struck his ankle. A copperhead connected on his other leg. Still, he lunged at Josh.

All I could do was scream as Josh fought off his father. He reached out in desperation, grabbing the only thing he could grab and drove a six-inch shard of glass into his father's neck.

Blood sprayed the walls as Raeford stumbled backwards, clutching the lethal weapon, unable to pull it out. In shock, Josh moved away from his father, pushing him, sending the man collapsing to his knees. Within seconds, the eastern diamondback Raeford had so lovingly handled earlier, struck and latched onto his cheek. He crumpled to the floor and landed face down in the thick coating of powder. The fine white crystals turned crimson as the powder soaked up Raeford's blood.

Frozen with fear, I couldn't move. Josh reached out for my hand. His hand was bleeding, sliced open from the shard of glass. "We've got to get out of here," he screamed. "The powder—it's Strychnine."

Don't breathe. Don't breathe. Don't breathe.

Arms outstretched, Josh screamed, "Jump!"

I couldn't peel my eyes away from Raeford, the snakes slithering and coiling around him, their bellies turning slick with blood.

"Ava jump. I've got you. We've got to get out of here."

I held my breath and jumped.

Josh grabbed me and shoved me out the door then slammed it shut. We rushed outside, each collapsing on the sharp gravel of the parking lot. I scrambled over to him, helping him to sit up. His hand was badly injured, cut to the tendons. I rushed to the Tahoe and dug a rag from the back then wrapped his hand to try and stop the bleeding. After I got the ends tied off, I called 911.

An hour later, I stood in a portable decontamination tent in the church parking lot, naked, numb. The Hazmat unit did allow me the dignity to strip down in the tent and not in the open for the world to see. A portable shower had been set up in the tent to wash away any remnants of the Strychnine. Josh was in a separate tent beside me. Our clothes had been bagged and sealed. While fire fighters in hazmat suits dealt with the poison inside the Higher Heavens Holiness Church, a detective with the Grayson County Sheriff's department waited patiently to speak with us. His boss, Sheriff Ray Tillman, talked quietly with several of his deputies.

Still in shock, I let the water wash over me, cleansing my memory of Raeford Bloom. The eyes. The smile. I closed my own eyes and imagined a baptism. My own.

"Miss Logan," Sheriff Tillman said outside the tent. "Sheriff Ridge is on his way. He should be here within the hour."

I looked skyward where just a short while ago a storm raged. Now a bright rainbow stretched across the Appalachian hills. Tears flowed freely and mingled with the water cleansing away the contaminant. I needed Grayson's strength right then more than ever. I needed his calm. I needed his arms around me.

Afterward, Josh and I sat on a bench like scolded children waiting to see the principal. Dressed in blaze orange jumpsuits and shower sandals borrowed from the local jail, we were surrounded by a flurry of activity. A crowd gathered beyond the crime scene tape sealing off the parking lot. The old men from the barber shop and the store clerk with the vacant eyes joined others in watching without speaking. Even Susan Bloom stood on the other side of the yellow line. Wearing her simple skirt and blouse, she wailed into the supportive arms of her church friends. I recognized them from the congregation. The lady who'd held the snake, the barber's wife who sat on the back row. Josh's little brother and sister clung to their mother's skirt, wide-eyed and frightened.

The detective from the Grayson County Sheriff's department squatted in front of us and spoke quietly. "Can you tell me what happened?"

I began but the pain ripping through my throat was too much. The screams, my screams, had stripped me of my voice, but not my memory. "Can I have some water?"

A moment later, another deputy brought me and Josh each

a cold bottle of water. After a couple of sips, the rawness had eased enough to speak a little. I told the story I'd never forget.

The detective turned to Josh. "Do you have proof your father killed your friend?"

Josh slowly nodded. "I was there," he whispered.

I jerked my head up. I knew why it happened, but through it all, I really hadn't learned *how* it happened.

"You want to tell me about it?" the detective asked.

Josh spoke so quietly it was hard to hear him. "We were in a relationship my father didn't approve of. Scott didn't understand my father's beliefs. He thought if he could talk to him...he might help him change his mind. He came to church that Sunday and told my father he wanted to talk to him afterward."

He stopped talking as I imagined visions he no longer wanted to see flashed through his mind. The detective prodded for more.

"After service, after everyone had left but me and my father, Scott started telling him how we felt about each other. Father wouldn't listen. He started shouting bible verses at us, calling Scott wicked." He took a drink of water then continued. "He lured Scott to the storage room and took out a couple of the snakes. Scott was scared and started yelling, calling father a freak. The snakes...bit several times. Scott was trying to fight them off and fell into one of the shelves. He hit his head. And the snakes just kept biting. I don't know if he was still alive then or not."

"Why didn't you call 911?"

Josh lifted his gaze from the ground to the detective. "God's our 911."

I returned the detective's glance. He then continued his

questioning, "what happened then?"

"Father made me help load his body in my truck and then we drove to Spearhead mountain. We buried him there."

The detective looked at me. "You can corroborate Reverend Bloom attacked his son in the storage room?"

I slowly nodded. But Scott wasn't buried. He was discarded like trash.

CHAPTER 26

Later that night I stood in the bedroom staring out the window into the darkness surrounding the river. The storm from earlier had dumped enough rain to make the river swell. The sound of the water moving downstream was always a constant, but tonight it sounded angry, almost violent.

My body ached all the way down to my bones from the stress of the day. The body aches would subside in a few days. It would be awhile before my mind let go of the shock. Although I now found comfort dressed in Grayson's Sheriff's Department sweatshirt and a pair of shorts, the thought of being stripped naked in front of strangers was unnerving. Even though I had been in the decontamination tent, I had felt bared, body and soul.

Grayson came in the bedroom and sat down on the side of the bed to remove his shoes. "Everyone's asleep and accounted for. Doors are locked. Finn and Boone are settled in for the night."

I left the window and the river behind and joined him. He draped his arm around my shoulder and pulled me in tight. His lips pressed against my forehead.

"Thank you for checking in on them," I whispered. My throat still ached from the strain.

"I didn't change Ivy's diaper. I left that for you."

I smiled despite the day I'd had. "I'm sure Emma put a clean one on her after her bath."

He laughed softly. "I didn't clean the litter box, either."

"S'okay. You're still my hero." I got up and tugged at his hands so I could pull the quilt back.

While I fixed the bed, he undressed down to his boxer briefs. He carefully folded his clothes and placed them on the settee then closed the bedroom door. I didn't want to admit or even think about how much I needed him.

I curled against him in bed. "What's going to happen to Josh?" I finally asked. The question had been lingering on the tip of my tongue all evening.

Grayson breathed in deeply. My hand rose and fell with the movement of his chest. "For Scott or his father?"

I gave it some thought, but after witnessing Raeford's death, no jury would find Josh guilty. "Both, I guess."

"He probably won't be charged for his father's death. With you there as a witness to back up his statement, it was clearly self-defense. In the end, it'll be up to the Grayson County District Attorney."

"And Scott?"

"That's trickier. We've got some jurisdictional issues since he was killed in Grayson County but dumped in Jackson County."

I propped up on my elbow and studied him. "I don't think *dumped* is the right word."

He cocked an eyebrow, knowing I knew the terminology. It just sounded obscene in this case. "He was killed in one location and his body moved to another. We call it a dump."

I sighed heavily, accepting it for what it was. "So, what's going to happen?"

"Grayson County could charge him with accessory, accessory after, obstruction of justice. There's several ways they could go with it."

I ran my finger over his chest, tracing tiny circles around his heart. "And you?"

"He concealed a body, Ava."

I eased back down beside him and rested my head on his chest. Our only arguments were always about the imaginary line he saw as rigid and I saw as bendable. "It's not always black and white."

"Laws are."

"Then why do y'all look the other way when snake handling churches are breaking the law?"

He took in a deep breath. "Religious freedom is a tricky subject."

I was too tired to engage in the debate, so I let it slide. Law or not, Josh did what he did with good intent.

"And oh—we got in touch with that bar Scott was at in Johnson City. A truck matching Josh's was seen on the security camera that night."

That made no sense. Quinn said Scott didn't leave with anyone. "Did they match the tags?"

"The tags weren't on camera."

"So you're not really sure it was his truck?"

Grayson pulled away then rolled over on his side to face me. "Why are you so convinced this kid's a good guy?"

I thought about it before answering. "Compared to his father, Satan himself was a good guy."

* * *

The next morning, the kids acted no different with Grayson there. He'd slept over two nights and they didn't react. Ivy was too young to know, Emma was old enough to question morals, and Cole was old enough to throw it in my face when he could use it in an argument. Despite the comments I imagined would come one day, it was nice waking up with him.

After dropping the kids at school, I took Ivy to Doretha's and lingered. She poured two cups of coffee and ordered me to sit at the dinette table in the kitchen while Ivy played. "You sure you feel up to working today?"

Truth was I didn't. I wanted nothing more than to stay at home and try to put my thoughts into something tangible. "I have a paper to get out. And a staff depending on me to do it."

The chicory coffee was bitter but strangely comforting. Like the circumstances of childhood. I was raised by Doretha in a happy home that I wasn't born into, yet I found comfort between these walls. The same hopefully would be said of Ivy and our home. Did Joshua Bloom find any amount of comfort in his childhood? When he thought back to days when he was younger, were they happy memories?

Doretha stirred her coffee. "We've rescheduled the baptism for Sunday after next. It won't be the big reunion like last time. Just a simple service."

A ping of guilt bubbled up. "I'll try not to interrupt this one."

Doretha cocked a brow then reached over and patted my hand. "You're forgiven. In hindsight, you were right to. You knew something was wrong when Scott didn't show up for work."

It still didn't lessen the fact I had put more thought into wondering what had happened than to being in the moment for my daughter. "What makes one religion believe one thing and another believes something totally different?"

"That's an age-old question, baby doll, with no easy answer."

"I mean, who's to say we're right and they're wrong?"

Doretha smiled in that all-knowing way she had. Even if she had the answer, she'd rather I discover it on my own.

I finished my coffee then gave Ivy a kiss and Doretha a hug. "I've got to get to the office. I've got an article to write."

Despite my earlier claim, Scott Curry had become a headline.

CHAPTER 27

I stared at the blank screen wondering how I was going to tell this story. The office bustled with normal activity: Nola dripping Southern charm with every phone call, my ad guy putting together a proposal, and Quinn cutting words from his article on Mary McCarter. Poor guy had to do an entire re-write after our visit to Fletcher Hanson. Carlyle Hanson had, for some reason, convinced Bob Palmer and the planning and zoning board to drop their investigation into Mary's home remedies. Turned out the embarrassment of a pill-popping wife having nearly killed their son was enough to make him play nice.

People came in and out of the office dropping off wedding announcements, or church fundraisers, or a cracked and faded picture taken fifty years ago of a young couple now celebrating a golden anniversary.

The news had not trickled down from Virginia yet, so the people that came in offered condolences on Scott's death, not shock over how he died. I didn't want to talk to anyone about it, so I offered little information. They could read about it in the paper. It would be a first-hand account.

With the chatter in the office getting on my nerves, I

slipped on a pair of headphones to drown out the conversations. Out of habit, I checked my cell phone before diving too deep into focused concentration. Grayson had called two hours ago. I checked my voicemail then hit "transcribe" to read it.

Josh is here in custody. I'll give you thirty minutes with him. I do love you.

I hurriedly logged off the computer then grabbed my bag. "Going to the sheriff's office," I whispered to Nola on my way out. I didn't wait for a response.

Rushing through town, a million thoughts ran through my head. Although we had sat beside one another while he told the detective what had happened, there was still so much I didn't know. I kept telling myself my need to know was so I could give Scott's story the justice it deserved, but I knew better.

I jerked the Tahoe into a parking space then rushed inside, not even stopping to say hello to Grayson's secretary, Annie. Straight to his office with Annie's voice trailing behind me. "He's expecting...you...."

Grayson's office door was open, so I went straight in. "Where is he?"

"He's in a holding cell. I'll have him brought up to an interview room."

I finally let out the breath I'd been holding since reading the message. "What's he charged with?"

He got up from behind his desk and walked over to me, hands in his pockets, rocking on the balls of his feet. That was his nervous way of contemplating what to say. "Obstruction of justice for starters."

"For starters? Grayson—"

He held his hand up to shush me. "He'll never do time, Ava. It'll probably be a suspended sentence or maybe even probation."

"What about Grayson County?"

He shook his head. "Self-defense. Come on. I'll walk you back."

Grayson escorted me through the hallway and into the same room where he'd told the Currys he'd found their son's body. I sat on the far side of the cheap table, facing the door. I tucked my hands under my legs to keep them from shaking. A laundry list of questions ticked off in my head. After a few minutes, Josh entered the room with Grayson behind him.

I wondered if the orange jumpsuit he wore was the same one the firemen gave us? The biggest difference was yesterday, his wrists weren't bound by handcuffs. Grayson pulled out a chair for Josh then one for himself. I hadn't realized Grayson was staying but I did understand why.

"Josh...I'm *so* sorry it ended like it did."

He placed his arms on the table and the cuffs thumped against the wood. "I'm not. Not really. My father wasn't the good soul he wanted everyone to believe he was."

My mind raced back to Mary McCarter's revelation of evil. It made sense now. Raeford Bloom and my father. The difference was my father never pretended he was good. "Why did you take Scott's body to Spearhead Mountain?"

"We had hiked it once. I knew how much he loved it there." He spoke in a faraway voice. He turned his eyes down to the table, to the handcuffs where his reflection gazed back in the polished steel. "Father wanted to burn the body. To stuff him in the burn barrel like we burn our trash. He got called away to a healing and that's when I moved the body–while he was gone."

I blinked once, twice. That wasn't what he'd told the detective at the church. I forced a deep breath, swallowed hard. I pushed my hands further under my legs. Maybe I'd misunderstood. The trauma of everything I'd just been through probably toyed with my memory. "How long were you and Scott involved before he came to church that Sunday?"

"Five, six months. I went...to his apartment...the week before Christmas break. Then he went back home, and I went home for the holiday. When we came back after the New Year, we knew we didn't want to have to do that again."

I didn't understand. "Do what?"

"Be separated."

"What happened then?"

For the first time since I'd met him, he smiled. A real, honest, from the heart smile. "We were happy. We hung out at his apartment a lot. Went down to Asheville some, Charlotte. You know, where we could be together without all the judging."

I thought of Quinn and how, even in this day and age of acceptance, I was the only one who knew his secret. And then I remembered what Quinn had said about seeing Scott at that club just last weekend. The night before he died. I glanced at Grayson, remembering Josh's truck was there, too.

Something didn't add up.

"Why did you move back home when school was finished? Why didn't you just stay with Scott?"

He grinned and shook his head. "That's not something you do in my family."

"So, were y'all not going to see each other over the summer break?"

He looked genuinely confused. "Yeah, I mean...we were. We just had some things to work out. He bought me a cell phone so we could keep in touch."

My breath hitched but Grayson never flinched. I asked, "Do

you still have the phone?"

Josh shook his head, twisted his lips. "Father found it and made me destroy it."

I prayed to God my face was a blank canvas instead of showing the confusion, and doubt, I felt. "When did you tell your father about Scott?"

Josh shrugged. I sensed he was tiring of the questions. "When he found the phone."

"When was that?"

"When he came to church with me. He wanted to tell Father about us, but I begged him not to. I knew how dangerous my father could be."

"Did he tell him?"

Josh stared at me without answering. Maybe he was taking time to figure out what he was going to say. Grayson's interest in his answers had grown as he leaned in closer to the table.

The pieces started coming together. The books on Scott's table about snakes, about poisons, and religion. Scott wasn't confessing his love for Josh at the church that day. He got a first-hand glimpse of what Higher Heavens Holiness Church was about and started back-peddling. He was moving as far away and as fast as he could from a den of vipers.

I rested my arms on the table, clasping my hands together, index fingers pointed like a steeple. "You didn't destroy the phone, did you Josh?"

His eyes narrowed and I fought off a chill. "What?"

"You didn't destroy the phone. We found it at Scott's. He took it back, didn't he?"

He leaned back in the chair, jaw jutted out defiantly. So different than the shy boy I first met stacking the stock at a tiny grocery store. The sincerity I had found in his tear-filled eyes had turned into a burning anger.

I swallowed the knot in the throat, nearly gagging on the truth. "Where were you Saturday night, Josh? The night before Scott was killed?"

He was taken aback at the question and frowned. "Why does that matter?"

"Were you at a bar in Johnson City, Tennessee?"

He guffawed. "A bar? Of course not."

"Scott was there. Maybe looking for a new relationship?"

Grayson eyed Josh cautiously as Josh opened and closed his hands into tight fists and clenched his jaw. "You don't know what you're talking about. I loved Scott."

"But he didn't love you back, did he Josh? That's why he went to the club. What'd you do? Follow him there?"

Josh bolted, lunging over the table. "Bitch!"

I leapt backward, knocking my chair over as Grayson dove on top of him. Within seconds, Steve Sullivan and two patrol officers were in the room wrestling Joshua Bloom to the ground. Grayson scrambled across the table and grabbed me, shielding me with his body.

Maybe he wasn't shielding me at all. Maybe he was holding me back. The anger rolling through me burned white hot. Raeford Bloom died at the hands of his own son. And Scott Curry died at the hands of psychopath.

CHAPTER 28

The rhododendron was in full bloom along the mountain roads as Quinn and I headed west to Scott's funeral. Not wanting to battle the wind through my hair again in Quinn's jeep, I drove. He cussed his phone and the lack of a signal from the passenger seat. "Damn mountains. Now I get why they used to use smoke signals."

I laughed. "They didn't exactly have cell towers back then. Who are you trying to call anyway?"

He grinned, and blushed. I'd never seen Quinn blush. "A friend."

I didn't press for more information, but I smiled, too.

He finally put away his phone with a degree of resignation. "So did they ever determine the cause of death?"

The question brought me back to the reality of where we were headed. "Multiple snake bites. He did have head trauma but not enough to have killed him."

"Do they know what really happened?"

I took a slow breath in and blew it out even slower. It all still seemed so unreal. I could still hear the tambourine, the stomping of the believers' feet as they danced, the babel spouting from their mouths. "The night you saw Scott at the bar, Josh was waiting on him in the parking lot and followed him home. They fought. Josh said Scott hit his head. He put him in the back of his truck and, quite by accident, the rattlers he had in the crate got loose."

"Because everyone drives around with crates full of poisonous snakes in the back of their truck. I believe that. Why didn't he call 911 when Scott fell?"

Because God's our 911—I could hear Josh say it again as if he were sitting beside me, whispering it in my ear. "Calling 911 shows a lack of faith."

Quinn stared at me a moment then turned back to watching the mountain laurel pass by. "At least he was unconscious when he was bitten."

I nodded. And hoped that was the case. I saw Raeford dying in front of me all over again. The rattler and copperhead striking out, fangs bared. The blood from the shard of glass glistening on the serpents' bellies.

Quinn asked, "Did they ever find Scott's car?"

"Bottom of a gorge a mile from his apartment."

We rode in silence the rest of way, each lost in our own thoughts. When we reached the small hillside cemetery, I parked behind a long row of cars already there. A crowd had gathered around a heavy canvas tent marked with a logo of Thomas Brother's Funeral Home. I stretched the kinks out of my legs before trekking up the hill to the gravesite. Mountains rose in the background, where the Blue Ridge met the Great Smokies, the blue haze mingling with the gray until you weren't sure which was which. Old-timers knew. They could point out the dividing line.

Like the imaginary line separating Scott's friends and

family. College-aged kids in torn jeans and printed t-shirts clustered together and laughed, shared stories, while Will and Lisa stood with their friends, neighbors probably, work associates. More somber, more traditionally dressed for a funeral. Sara sat by herself in one of the chairs lined up in front of the grave.

With a few minutes before the service was scheduled to start, I slid into the seat beside Sara. She glanced up and smiled softly. "You kept your promise."

I wasn't sure I understood, and my questioning expression must have relayed that. "You said you'd find out what happened to him. And you did."

I reached out and took her hand. "I'm so sorry it didn't have a happier ending."

She inhaled deeply and held it a moment, then nodded. "Dad's still in denial."

"You mean about the relationship?"

She nodded again. "I think that was harder for him to accept than the fact he was murdered."

She leaned her head on my shoulder and we sat like that until the service began. I moved to the back row of chairs and sat beside Quinn. The preacher wore an ill-fitting suit a size too small. His comb-over made me want to cut his hair and tell him no, just no. Nothing about him resonated with me the way Raeford Bloom had.

I had vastly different beliefs than Raeford, but I could see how a person could be drawn in. Terrorized and mesmerized at the same time. The markings of a psychopath. Maybe Josh got it honestly?

After the service, I spoke to Will and Lisa and offered my condolences. Lisa clung to my hand like she was afraid of letting go of a small part of her son's life. "We want to subscribe to the paper. Do you do mailed subscriptions?"

I squeezed her hand and smiled tenderly. "I'll add you to the database."

CHAPTER 29

Emma stood with four others in the chilly water of Jackson Creek professing their faith, their white robes ballooning around them. Doretha shouted praises to heaven then dunked one after the other. The water flowed clear this time, leaving only a water line on their robes and not mud.

This time there was no picnic, no banjo picking, and no one there but the immediate families of the new believers. Us and two others were the only blood families; the other two were Doretha's kids.

We stood on the bank close enough to the water that Grayson held Ivy. I didn't ask him to; he just did. And this time Cole didn't beg to see Paisley, because she was with us. They stood a few feet from us, holding hands, whispering to one another. Like young love should be.

When it was Emma's turn, she looked up at us and smiled with her whole face. Doretha recited a verse then asked Emma something. They burst out laughing then Emma nodded excitedly. She crossed her arms, held her nose with one hand, then disappeared as Doretha lowered my daughter beneath the water. A second later, she sprang up, busting through the surface and raised her arms to heaven.

I didn't know if she truly understood the meaning, and I didn't care. She was happy in her belief. It still puzzled me how people who believed in the same God could be so far apart in the ways they worshiped.

When all the new believers had been baptized, Grayson handed Ivy to me and helped Doretha out of the water. I thought for a moment in her struggle, she was going to pull him in.

"Lord, help us all," she said when she finally made it up on the bank. "These ol' knees are a hurting!" Although in pain, she laughed.

I helped Emma out of the wet robe then gave her a heavy towel. I held the same old quilt up so she could change clothes. The memory of the decontamination tent sprang through my mind and I quickly shut it out. *Not today*. This was Emma's day. I glanced over at Doretha. "What were y'all laughing at in the river?"

They both started laughing again then Doretha said, "you don't want to know."

I gave Emma the stink eye, demanding an answer. "Don't get mad," she said through a chuckle. "Doretha said she was going to make this one fast in case you went crazy again."

They both laughed so hard they snorted. I rolled my eyes but smiled despite myself.

Later at the house, Paisley helped me set the table for a celebration dinner. She was a good kid. I couldn't find anything to dislike about her and I did try. I wanted to shield Cole from the broken heart I knew would come when they both moved on to someone new. I wanted to be able to tell him she wasn't good for him, but she was.

More than once today Raeford Bloom crossed my mind. I

didn't believe in his ways, but did it really make him a horrible person? My father and Joshua Bloom were evil. Raeford Bloom wasn't. He just believed what he believed.

Paisley came into the kitchen from the dining room holding the stack of mail, homework papers and the newspapers that tended to collect on the formal table. "Where do you want me to put these?"

"You can just put them on the counter." In other words, move them from one location to the other until I scan through them and toss most.

She put the stack on the counter then carried the plates into the dining room. Although I'd read it a thousand times—I'd even written it—I couldn't stop staring at the copy of the *Jackson Creek Chronicle* laying on top of the pile.

Virginia Man Charged with Murder in the Death of Scott Curry. Front page. Above the fold.

LYNN CHANDLER WILLIS

Lynn Chandler Willis has worked in the corporate world, the television industry, and owned a small-town newspaper (much like Ava Logan). She's lived in North Carolina her entire life and couldn't imagine living anywhere else. Her novel, a Shamus Award finalist, *Wink of an Eye*, won the SMP/PWA Best 1st PI Novel competition, making her the first woman in a decade to win the national contest. Her debut novel, *The Rising*, won the Grace Award for Excellence in Faith-based Fiction.

The Ava Logan Mystery Series
by Lynn Chandler Willis

TELL ME NO LIES (#1)
TELL ME NO SECRETS (#2)
TELL ME YOU LOVE ME (#3)

Henery Press Mystery Books

And finally, before you go...
Here are a few other mysteries
you might enjoy:

COUNTERFEIT CONSPIRACIES

Ritter Ames

A Bodies of Art Mystery (#1)

Laurel Beacham may have been born with a silver spoon in her mouth, but she has long since lost it digging herself out of trouble. Her father gambled and womanized his way through the family fortune before skiing off an Alp, leaving her with more tarnish than trust fund. Quick wits and connections have gained her a reputation as one of the world's premier art recovery experts. The police may catch the thief, but she reclaims the missing masterpieces.

The latest assignment, however, may be her undoing. Using every ounce of luck and larceny she possesses, Laurel must locate a priceless art icon and rescue a co-worker (and ex-lover) from a master criminal, all the while matching wits with a charming new nemesis. Unfortunately, he seems to know where the bodies are buried—and she prefers hers isn't next.

KILLER IMAGE

Wendy Tyson

An Allison Campbell Mystery (#1)

As Philadelphia's premier image consultant, Allison Campbell helps others reinvent themselves, but her most successful transformation was her own after a scandal nearly ruined her. Now she moves in a world of powerful executives, wealthy, eccentric ex-wives and twisted ethics.

When Allison's latest Main Line client, the fifteen-year-old Goth daughter of a White House hopeful, is accused of the ritualistic murder of a local divorce attorney, Allison fights to prove her client's innocence when no one else will. But unraveling the truth brings specters from her own past. And in a place where image is everything, the ability to distinguish what's real from the facade may be the only thing that keeps Allison alive.

SHADOW OF DOUBT

Nancy Cole Silverman

A Carol Childs Mystery (#1)

When a top Hollywood Agent is found poisoned in her home, suspicion quickly turns to one of her two nieces. But Carol Childs, a reporter for a local talk radio station doesn't believe it. The suspect is her neighbor and friend, and also her primary source for insider industry news. When a media frenzy pits one niece against the other—and the body count starts to rise—Carol knows she must save her friend from being tried in courts of public opinion.

But even the most seasoned reporter can be surprised, and when a Hollywood psychic shows warns Carol there will be more deaths, things take an unexpected turn. Suddenly nobody is above suspicion. Carol must challenge both her friendship and the facts, and the only thing she knows for certain is the killer is still out there and the closer she gets to the truth, the more danger she's in.

MURDER ON A SILVER PLATTER

Shawn Reilly Simmons

A Red Carpet Catering Mystery (#1)

Penelope Sutherland and her Red Carpet Catering company just got their big break as the on-set caterer for an upcoming blockbuster. But when she discovers a dead body outside her house, Penelope finds herself in hot water. Things start to boil over when serious accidents threaten the lives of the cast and crew. And when the film's star, who happens to be Penelope's best friend, is poisoned, the entire production is nearly shut down.

Threats and accusations send Penelope out of the frying pan and into the fire as she struggles to keep her company afloat. Before Penelope can dish up dessert, she must find the killer or she'll be the one served up on a silver platter.

CPSIA information can be obtained
at www.ICGtesting.com
Printed in the USA
BVHW072253270619
R10061500001B/R100615PG551797BVX20B/3/P